WITCHY WHISKERS

A NINE LIVES MAGIC MYSTERY

DANIELLE GARRETT

ROOTS & WINGS
PRESS

BOOKS BY DANIELLE GARRETT

BEECHWOOD HARBOR MAGIC MYSTERIES

Murder's a Witch

Twice the Witch

Witch Slapped

Witch Way Home

Along Came a Ghost

Lucky Witch

Betwixt: A Beechwood Harbor Collection

One Bad Witch

A Royal Witch

First Place Witch

Sassy Witch

The Witch Is Inn

Men Love Witches

Goodbye's a Witch

BEECHWOOR HARBOR GHOST MYSTERIES

The Ghost Hunter Next Door

Ghosts Gone Wild

When Good Ghosts Get the Blues

Big Ghosts Don't Cry

Diamonds are a Ghost's Best Friend

Ghosts Just Wanna Have Fun

Bad Ghosts Club

Mean Ghosts

SUGAR SHACK WITCH MYSTERIES

Sprinkles and Sea Serpents

Grimoires and Gingerbread

Mermaids and Meringue

Sugar Cookies and Sirens

Hexes and Honey Buns

Leprechauns and Lemon Bars

NINE LIVES MAGIC MYSTERIES

Witchy Whiskers

Hexed Hiss-tory

Cursed Claws

Purr-fect Potions

Furry Fortunes

Talisman Tails

Stray Spells

Mystic Meow

Catnip Charms

Yuletide Yowl

Paw-ful Premonition

Growling Grimoire

MAGIC INN MYSTERIES

Witches in the Kitchen

Fairies in the Foyer

Ghosts in the Garden

HAVEN PARANORMAL ROMANCES

Once Upon a Hallow's Eve

A TOUCH OF MAGIC MYSTERIES

Cupid in a Bottle

Newly Wed and Slightly Dead

Couture and Curses

Wedding Bells and Deadly Spells

The sun sank toward the jagged mountain range bordering Winterspell's north-western edge. Its red-gold light reflected off the crystal-clear lake in the center of town, turning it into a pool of amber fire. Wistfully, I stared out the window from my place behind the cash register and stifled an impatient sigh. There were only twenty minutes to closing, and on another night I might have closed early and headed to the lake to soak up the tail end of the sunset, but tonight my magical candle shop, Wicked Wicks, was unusually busy with half a dozen customers still perusing the display shelves. Even after ringing up everyone's purchases and shepherding the last of them out the door, I'd still need to tidy up the sales floor. No matter how careful or diligent my clientele were, inevitably merchandise got put back in the wrong place, and sometimes even damaged or broken. By the time I finished, the sun would be gone.

Maybe tomorrow I'd have better luck. In any case, I couldn't complain. Being an entrepreneur had its challenges, but I was fortunate to own a successful shop in a small town, and from a quick glance around the shop, it looked as though I'd have another run of sales to cap off the day. Besides, a quiet night in didn't sound too bad. Earlier that afternoon, Shanna, one of the fairies who worked at the Winterspell library, had popped over to let me know two of my hold requests had come in. I could stop by on my bike ride home and pick them up, then maybe grab something from Whimzee's Delicatessen. I'd tell myself I would only read a few chapters and get to sleep at a decent hour, but I knew that was a lie. That was part of the thrill of it, getting sucked into a juicy chapter right before bed.

A young man approached the counter and caught my attention. He looked in his late teens, with a lanky build and a mop of sandy blond hair that looked a good few weeks past due for a cut. Then again, maybe that was the in-style look these days. I was only thirty-four years old, but my own teen years may as well have been a millennium ago according to this new generation.

I smiled politely. "Can I help you?"

The young man raked his fingers through the hair falling across his forehead. "Maybe," he said. "Do you have any candles that can make you dream about being something, like, well, maybe like a superhero?"

Without missing a beat, I skirted around the short counter and went to a colorful display near the window. I picked up two different candles, one red, one blue. "Are you a Marvel guy, or DC?"

"Um, DC. Batman, specifically, I guess," the young man said. I extended the blue candle toward him, and his brows lifted as he took it from me. He turned it over in his hand, inspecting the waxy exterior. "So, this thing really works, huh?"

I laughed softly. "I offer a money-back guarantee. Burn it for at least thirty minutes before you go to sleep, think Batman thoughts, or read one of your favorite comics, and I promise you'll be protecting Gotham City as soon as you close your eyes."

The teen gave an appreciative nod at the candle, and then lifted his aqua-blue eyes up to me, a hint of pink appearing on his cheeks. "Any chance I might meet Catwoman in this dream?"

Aha. I suppressed a knowing grin. "The magic works with your imagination, sort of feeding off your conscious thoughts and then opening the gateway for it to play out in your dreams. I can't promise anything specific beyond the intention of the candle, in this case, superhero."

"Cool." Satisfied, he tucked the candle under his arm and followed me back to the register. I rang him up and sent him on his way. No sooner had he left than another customer approached the counter. A middle-aged woman held up a sparkling black tapered candle. "Do you have any more of these night sky candles?"

My lips quirked to one side as I peered past the woman and saw that the candle's designated basket was indeed empty. "The Celestial Starscape is one of my most popular candles," I said as I returned my gaze to the woman. "Generally, I keep all of my inventory on the floor, but I'll go see if I have any extras in the back."

"Don't bother," the woman said, her expression sour. "At these prices I shouldn't buy two, anyway. I'll just break this one in half."

I shook my head. "I'm afraid that won't work. It's intended to burn as it is. If you'd like, I do offer a customer loyalty program. If you spend—"

"Ugh, save it," the woman scoffed.

I smiled through my incredulity as the woman tossed the candle back into a basket—the wrong one —and left the store empty handed.

Some people just liked to complain. It was one of the inevitable truths of working retail. I'd learned to accept it. Mostly.

As the woman left, another customer walked in. She was a young mother with a baby on one hip, and a small child following after her, talking excitedly about the airplane toy he held overhead as he marched along behind his mom.

I knew what she wanted before she even had to ask, and with a smile, I pulled a box out from underneath the register. "I snagged these for you before I sold out again," I told her.

"Oh, may the goddess bless you!" she exclaimed as she rushed to the counter. She plopped her baby daughter next to the register and dug into her crossbody bag to dig out her wallet.

I smiled and started ringing up the purchase. Lydia was one of my regulars. She came in most Thursday afternoons to stock up on relaxation candles. She'd told me once that her mother-in-law watched her two young kids on weekend afternoons and she used the time to recharge her batteries. Hence the candles.

Lydia and I made small talk for a couple of minutes, then she hurried away, waving back at me as she passed by the front window, on the way to her next errand.

"At least the little brat didn't break anything this time," a cold voice said behind me.

Frowning, I turned to the gray-furred leonine form lounging atop the display case behind the cash register. The cat's ears went back. "Why haven't you kicked these people out of here so we can leave?"

"That's not how this works, Selene," I replied, keeping my voice low. "These are my customers. It's my job to help make sure they get everything they need."

"Please," she scoffed, adding a flick of her tail for emphasis. "This modern notion of customer service is so tiresome. You go to a shop in Europe, they treat you like total crap. And the customers know better than to complain. It's just expected."

I rolled my eyes. "Well, this isn't Europe. If I started acting like that, I could kiss my business goodbye."

"I doubt that. Just look at all these fools. Buying

your silly candles to create the same effect as a plastic projector from IKEA."

I shot the cat a scowl. Selene was being crotchety and exaggerating, as usual. The fact was, my Celestial Starscape candle did a lot more than simply "project" the image of a night sky across a wall. It created a magical illusion synced to the night sky, one so detailed and dynamic it truly made one feel like they were floating far above the earth watching the celestial seas ebb and flow.

But Selene liked to argue, and I refused to give in to her baiting. So, rather than try to explain how my magic candles worked for the umpteenth time, I ignored her and went to circle the shop, checking in with the handful of remaining customers. I rang up a few more sales before the clock reached the top of the hour. A soft chime rippled through the shop, signaling it was now closing time. My regulars knew what the sound meant, but out-of-towners and tourists mostly ignored it.

Two more customers filtered out without purchasing anything, and I went to clean up the shelves where they'd been looking before winding back to my last remaining customer. I'd noticed him from the moment he'd walked through my door. For one thing, he was wearing a three-piece suit, something of a rarity in our casual lakeside town. On top of that, he was one of the most handsome men I'd seen in Winterspell. He had thoughtful eyes that moved through the store with intense scrutiny. Though, if he'd noticed me at all, it was only in a passing glance. He'd been perusing the aisles unassisted for the last half hour and seemed lost in his own thoughts as he moved amongst the other customers. But now we were alone—well, save for Selene, and she'd better keep her big mouth closed. I'd be mortified if she came down from her perch to start hassling the man into leaving the shop now that we were officially closed for the night.

With a little flutter of nerves, I approached the man in the suit and cleared my throat softly. "Did you have any questions I could answer?"

His dark brown eyes darted over to me and took in the fact I was wearing a sales apron.

My stomach sank a little as I realized he held one of my Date Night candles. I quickly gave myself a mental kick for being disappointed. Of course he had a love interest.

He glanced around the shop as if only just realizing he was the last customer left. He quickly brought his attention back to me. "Erm, yes, actually, I probably could use some advice," he said. His voice had a velvet, honeyed quality that felt warm and inviting.

"Of course!" I replied, a little too eagerly.

Selene noticed. "Oy, we're never getting out of here," she muttered from her perch.

The man's brows rose.

"Ignore her," I said, flapping a dismissive hand back toward the register.

"Right. Um, well, I'm looking to put together a gift for my mother," he continued. "You've got a lot of interesting options here, and I want to make sure I find something she would like."

"Oh!" I smiled and gestured at the candle he clasped with one hand. "In that case, I think you might want to put that one back."

"Really?" His face contorted in a frown as he stared at the candle. "I picked this one up because pink is her favorite color."

"Hmm, well, that might be the case, but that candle has a very specific effect. It's meant to increases the, uh, the libido."

I laughed softly as the man's eyes went wide and he treated the candle like a hot potato, nearly dropping it before swiftly replacing it on the shelf.

"I don't think she's going to go for that, no," he said, accepting my laugh with good grace. "I'm in town visiting, and I guess I didn't fully realize how this all worked."

"No problem. I get a lot of tourists in here. I would have checked in with you sooner, but it's been a little busy this evening." I turned my body to draw attention back to the shelves before us. "All of the candles are magically imbued and have a specific purpose. Some of them are meant to create an atmosphere or set a specific mood. Others are meant to be burned before going to bed, to create certain types of dreams."

"Wow. That's impressive," he remarked. "I'll confess, I live outside the magical world, so I sometimes forget things like this are even possible."

"Where do you live?"

"Chicago," he replied with a short nod. "I'm a business consultant."

"I've never been. Do you like it?"

"It has its perks. But then, there's no magic candle shops there," he said with a chuckle.

I smiled, and when his eyes found mine, they seemed to really take me in for the first time. "I'm Clint Bridges," he said, offering his hand to me.

I shook it once. "Cora Hearth."

"Nice to meet you, Cora. So, you think you can help me find just the right candle for my mother?"

"Most definitely. Let me show you some of my other stock, though. Most of the items here are made with romance in mind." I gestured for him to follow, and we walked around to the other side of the shelf. "It might help if you told me a little bit about your mother."

"She's an earth witch, and, um, she likes bird watching, and …" Clint trailed off for a moment, then sighed. "Sorry. This is a lot harder than I thought. You see, I actually haven't seen my mother in quite a few years."

"No problem. I'm sure we can find something." I plucked a green candle from the shelf. Dried hibiscus petals were nestled in the wax around the wick. "This is a really popular one around Mother's Day. Burning this one will fill a small room with the illusion of a tropical waterfall. Everything will look, sound, and smell like you're right at the base of some remote waterfall in Hawaii, with little twinkling faerie lights blinking all around."

"That sounds great," he said. "I can't believe I've never heard of this kind of thing before."

I smiled. "I can't claim to be the first witch to capture illusions in candle wax, but I do work really hard to make sure I include as many olfactory and auditory elements as I can within each of my products."

Clint stared at the candle with reverence.

Smiling, I hitched one shoulder. "Sometimes I tell people to think of it like the holodeck from *Star Trek*."

"*That* I understand," Clint said, laughing softly.

"Aha, a fellow nerd," I teased. "Tell you what. How about a little demonstration?"

"Oh, sure, it's not like you're cutting into someone's dinner time," Selene complained from across the room.

"Yes, well unless *someone* wants to eat dry kitty kibble for the next week, *someone* better pipe down," I called over my shoulder before taking the candle from Clint's hand with a determined set to my jaw.

"Are you sure?" Clint asked, his gaze darting past my left shoulder for a flicker of a moment. "I really don't have to keep you any longer."

"It's more than fine," I told him. "Selene is perfectly capable of finding her own dinner. She's just fussy and spoiled."

Clint still looked a little unsure, but he followed me to the front counter where I kept a silver display candelabra for just such an occasion. I set the waterfall candle in place and lit a match. The wick caught and the candle sparked to life. For a moment, nothing changed, then a whisper of a breeze swirled through the shop.

"It smells like hibiscus," Clint said, tilting his chin up. "Is that the flowers or the magic? How long does it take to—"

The walls, shelves, and merchandise vanished. Clint and I now stood in a tropical cove, surrounded by lush greenery and a slick rocky wall on three sides. Behind Clint the falls rushed into the pool of crystal-clear water below, and soft fairy lights twinkled over our heads, like giant lightning bugs among the foliage.

"Wow. This is … this is really impressive." Clint's voice held a note of genuine admiration that pleased me. "What happens if I try to walk around? Will I bump into a shelf?"

I shook my head. "No, your mind is fooled into walking around them. My candles are one hundred percent safe. The range isn't too much bigger than the space of the shop, and if you were to go through the door, the illusion would break for you before you could accidentally stumble out into traffic."

Clint walked around, testing the boundaries of

the spell, before returning to my side. This time he stood a little closer, and for a moment even I got caught up in the illusion. Clint smiled down at me, his deep brown eyes gleaming. "This is incredible. You have a really special talent, Cora."

"Thank you," I said, letting myself bask in it for a moment longer before snuffing the candle out. The illusion faded almost instantly, and we were once again in my cozy, if not overstuffed, little shop.

Clint shook his head, still marveling at the whole experience. "That was amazing. I'm definitely getting her this candle. What else do you have?" He reached for a display of persimmon-colored globes the size of softballs. "Night Spice? What does this one do?"

I tucked my lips together for a moment, suppressing the urge to giggle.

Clint quirked a brow.

Gently, I took it from his hand and set it back on the display. "Let's just say it gives dreams of an, um, amorous nature?"

"Wow, I sure can pick them, can't I?" Clint laughed once again. I liked his laugh. It was unforced, and he wasn't afraid to direct it at himself. "It's a good thing I'm in the hands of an expert."

I felt my cheeks flush. The chemistry with Clint was definitely there. It had been a long time since I had felt the peculiar thrill of excitement that came from a bit of flirting. My last few dates had left much to be desired in the departments of charm and savoir faire. Clint was a refreshing change.

"I promise not all of my candles are intended for honeymooners," I teased lightly, as I snagged a candle on the opposite end of the display from the Night Spice. "She might like this one. It creates an illusion of the Venice Canal from the point of view of a gondola floating down the famed waterways. You also said she likes pink. I have one over here that creates a field of lavender at dusk. It's not hot pink, but kind of a rosebud pink."

Clint followed me around the shop, agreeing to all of my suggestions, and after ten minutes we'd managed to fill an entire wicker shopping basket. As I added in the last of my citrus grove candles, I realized I'd never asked what his budget was for the gift. Granted, judging by the looks of his tailored suit, loafers, and carefully coiffed hair, he wasn't hurting for money.

After depositing the candle, I clasped my hands together in front of me. "Well, what do you think?"

"I think I need to tell my personal trainer we need to work on my endurance," Clint jested, making a show of heaving the overloaded basket onto the counter before grabbing his biceps in jest.

I laughed and scurried to get back behind the register. Dusk had officially fallen over the small town, and after a quick glance at the clock, I realized I'd missed my window to stop by the library and pick up my holds. Somehow, I didn't mind all that much anymore.

"I think you've made some great choices," I told Clint as I started totaling up the order. "Your mother is a lucky lady to have such a thoughtful son."

Something flickered in Clint's eyes, and he looked out the front window for a long moment.

Sensing I'd stepped on some kind of emotional landmine, I busied myself with getting a paper bag ready.

"Aren't you going to upsell this into a gift basket?" Selene interjected.

I straightened. "I, uh—"

"If you're going to make me wait all night, you might as well get your full money's worth out of the sap," the cat groused.

Clint shifted his attention back to me. I was about to scold Selene for being so rude—not that it would make a difference—but to my surprise, instead of being offended, Clint laughed. "A gift basket sounds like just what this *sap* needs."

"I am so sorry about her," I whispered. "You really don't have to—"

"No, no. I insist. That is, if you have the time. I know I've already kept you."

I knew my cheeks were a bright shade of pink as I set about wrapping the candles and arranging them into a large basket. "I don't mind."

Selene looked on with feline judgement as I finished arranging the basket. In total, Clint's order came to over two hundred dollars, a sum that far exceeded my typical order. Even if he weren't handsome and charming, I would have been happy to stay well past closing for the sale alone. He flashed a black credit card and I ran it through. While we waited for the receipt to print, Clint thanked me once more for my assistance.

"You're very welcome," I replied, smiling as I handed him the receipt.

He tucked it into the inside pocket of his suit jacket, matching my smile. "I know I've already asked a lot of you, but—"

"Oh, boy. Here we go," Selene sighed.

Undeterred, Clint pressed on, "—I'd be grateful if you could give me a recommendation for dinner."

"Oh." I blinked. "Sure! There's quite a few good places in town. It sort of depends on what you're in the mood for. Whimzee's Deli is great for fast and easy. Um, there's Elephant's Palace, which has great Indian cuisine."

"Mmm, that sounds like it could hit the spot."

"It's just a few shops down from here," I said, gesturing out the front window in the direction of the restaurant. "They're open for another three hours."

"Is there any chance you might be free to join me, now that you've gotten rid of your last annoying customer?" Clint asked with a shy half-smile.

Selene flew over my shoulder and landed with a light *thump* on the counter. "Unless my eyesight is failing, it looks like he's still here," she commented, glowering up at Clint with her bright blue eyes.

Great. My first decent dinner date invitation in months and my mouthy familiar was going to chase him off just to spite me. Generally speaking, a familiar was meant to assist a witch, to be her helper and confidant. Selene was interested in none of those things. She had two modes: sarcastic and grumpy, and even on her best day she wouldn't so much as twitch a whisker to help me out of a bind.

I jabbed the tip of my finger against her hind quarter.

"I'd be delighted," I told Clint, hoping it struck the right balance between enthusiasm and casualness. The last thing I wanted was to sound desperate.

"Great! Let me go put this in my car, and we can walk over to the restaurant."

Nodding, I turned and began pulling my apron off over my head. "That sounds—"

The chime on the front door interrupted me, and I raised my voice, not really looking at the new would-be patron. "I'm sorry, but we just closed."

"Closed? Surely you can make an exception for me."

The sound of the all-too-familiar voice sent my heart plunging to the bottom of my stomach faster than an elevator car with a snapped cable.

Swinging around, my jaw dropped at the sight of the blue-eyed man standing in the entrance of the shop with his hands in his front pockets.

Somehow, I managed to get out a single word. "Roger?"

"Honey, I'm home," he said, his smile failing as his gaze darted to Clint and then back to me.

My magic candles could temporarily alter reality, but when the wick sputtered and the flame died out, real life was always there waiting on the other side of the illusion. This was especially true when it came to Roger. There wasn't a spell I could cast to scrub away his memory. All the magic in the world couldn't get rid of one's ex-husband.

2

Seeing Roger again felt like the emotional equivalent of popping the top off one of those cans of fake peanut brittle. Only, instead of spring-loaded rubber snakes, I was hit in the face by a full-on tsunami of memories.

"Um, what are you doing here, Roger?" I asked as my fingers toyed with the shred of leftover wrapping paper left on the counter. I swallowed hard and hoped my expression didn't reveal the panicked way my heart was beating in my chest.

"It's good to see you, too, Cora," Roger replied with a quick grin. "I thought you might be a little more excited to see me."

Before I could reply, Clint turned and gestured

for his gift basket, his expression a little hurt. "Seems like maybe we need to put a pin in that dinner."

"Dinner, huh?" Roger said, cocking an eyebrow in my direction. "Is this guy a customer or your boyfriend?"

Selene perked up. "Ooh. Are you two going to fight?'

"No one is going to fight," I snapped. Pitching the scrap paper into the trash basket, I exhaled. "Clint, this is my ex-husband, Roger."

There. That should be the final nail in that particular coffin. Oh well, it was fun while it lasted anyway.

"Clint?" Roger repeated, taking a lumbering step toward him. He sized him up, which felt a little caveman and unnecessary, especially considering they were almost the same height. The difference between them was that Roger had a swimmer's build, with broad shoulders and a trim waist, whereas Clint was slimmer overall, but was likely not too far off Roger's weight.

"I see," Clint said, offering a brief smile as he inclined his head in a polite nod.

"And you're Cora's ... what, exactly?"

"Roger, that really isn't any of your—"

"New friend," Clint replied.

"Uh huh." Roger's smile seemed genial enough. "Nice suit. You work at the bank or something?"

"Ugh, this is boring," Selene complained. She jumped down from the front counter and marched to the front door. Despite her demands, I still hadn't installed a cat flap, so she was forced to wait until someone opened it for her. With an expectant huff, she shifted her icy glare up at Roger. "Hey, you with the untucked shirt, make yourself useful and open this door."

"Since when are you a cat person?" Roger asked me.

I shot Selene a dark look. "Believe me, I'm not."

Selene's tail swished. "You're not a cat person, I'm not a witch cat."

"Wait! I know where I've seen you before. You belonged to Cora's crazy aunt!"

Selene's eyes went pure glacier as she glared up at Roger, then flicked her tail and a *crack* snapped through the air. The pulse of magic wasn't powerful enough to actually harm someone, or cause damage to anything in the shop, but it had its intended result as Roger flinched and took a few steps back from the tiny ten-pound feline.

Selene flashed her teeth in a satisfied smirk.

"I'll get the door," Clint said, hurrying to gather

the large gift basket. "Thank you again for your help, Cora. Maybe I'll see you around before I leave town."

My heart twisted as he turned his back. "Here, let me help." I walked out from behind the counter, keeping my stride quite calm in spite of the storm brewing in my belly. Likewise, my facial expression remained inscrutable as I nudged past Roger to the front door of my shop. As soon as I pushed it open, Selene made a run for it, streaking down the sidewalk without a backward glance. Clint nodded at me as he passed through. When the door shut, I flipped the OPEN sign around to the CLOSED side and exhaled.

"Who was that guy?" Roger asked.

"How is that any of your business, Roger?"

"Hey, I was just stopping in to say hey, and see if you wanted to grab dinner." He held out his hands. "No big deal."

"And what about that big, loud 'hey, honey, I'm home'?"

"It was just a joke, Cora."

"A joke?" I sputtered. "Roger, I haven't seen or heard from you in eighteen months. You can't just barge in here and pretend like not a moment has passed and expect me to drop everything and spend time with you."

"You make it sound like me wanting to spend time with you is a bad thing." A mixture of hurt and confusion flashed in his eyes, but my anger remained unabated.

"We're not together anymore! If we wanted to spend time together, then we'd probably still be married."

"Come on, Cora, we both know it's not as simple as all that." Roger's tone softened. "Besides, that's all water under the bridge, now. Would it really be terrible to have dinner, maybe catch up?"

I didn't have an answer for him, so I retreated behind the counter, emotions roiling in my gut for dominance. "Why didn't you at least call me first?" A new thought popped into my head, and I cringed. "Is everyone all right?"

Roger left Winterspell before the ink on our divorce papers had fully dried, but his entire family still lived here. Seeing as it wasn't the holidays, I hoped his abrupt return hadn't been spurred by a family member's illness, or the goddess forbid, death.

"Everyone's good," he assured me. After a moment, his gaze fell to the wooden surface between us, and my heart jolted once more. It was clear this wasn't how he envisioned this meeting.

The valve on my frustration released, and I exhaled along with it. "I'm glad to hear it."

He met my eyes again as he looked down at me. Almost everyone was taller than me. It was one of those things that came along with being a card-carrying member of the short girls club. Roger was just over six foot, which gave him a solid ten inches on me. It had been the point of many jokes between us back when we were together. I used to tease him that the only reason I kept him around was because he was tall enough to reach the stuff on the top shelf at the grocery store.

Roger smiled. "It's good to see you, Cora."

Despite myself, I allowed a nod of agreement.

Our marriage had ended amicably enough. No hurled dinnerware, no broken windows or torched vehicles. Just a mutual acknowledgment that we'd drifted apart during our four-year union. When Roger got a job offer in New York City, that was the final straw. He wanted to take the job. I didn't want to move, and so I'd suggested, almost casually over pasta one night, that we should get a divorce.

There had been a few tears on both of our parts, but it never turned into a full-blown sobfest. Even after he moved out of our home and left town, I never fell into the "eat nothing but Ben & Jerry's on the couch" phase. Instead, there was just a lingering sense of sadness, a mourning for what might have been.

I'd worked hard to put that part of my life in the rearview mirror and live in the present, but having Roger walk in the door of my shop dredged up all of those memories and feelings in an instant.

I took a sidestep and planted myself behind the register. I needed to be doing something with my hands. "How have things been going? How's the new job?" I asked as I pressed a series of buttons to print the day's sales report.

Roger's face scrunched up into a grimace. His eyes grew hard as he turned toward the window. "The new job is no more." His shoulders deflated as he let out a long sigh. "That's the problem with star-tups. Things go along great until they don't. When I started, the company rented three floors in an office building and all of them were filled with workers. Last month, right before it went under, we were down to less than a dozen employees."

"I'm sorry," I said, and meant it. I never would have wished failure or misery on Roger. The memory of our love was more than enough to prevent such pettiness. "I really am. I know you had high hopes for that job."

"It is what it is," Roger said. "The truth is, I'm not sure I would have been happy there even if the job had worked out."

I thought about asking him to elaborate, but quickly decided against it. A tapping sounded on the glass door, and Roger turned. Selene glared at him and tapped twice more with her paw.

Sighing, I nudged my chin toward the cat. "Might as well open it for her. She's more stubborn than your father."

Roger chuckled as he moved to let her inside. "Impressive. I figured he held the world record."

Selene stalked inside, her tail held aloft. "Cora, you're going to have to settle your bill with the fish market. They're cutting me off until you do. The audacity!"

My brows peaked. "How is that possible? We have a two-hundred-dollar cap, and I just paid it off three weeks ago!"

"Caviar doesn't come cheap," Selene said, twitching her whiskers as she gracefully leaped back onto the counter and settled herself next to the register. "What's this oaf still doing here? You're not really considering going out to dinner with him, are you? At least the other one didn't slap a shaggy caterpillar on his upper lip and call it a mustache."

Selene's commentary usually irked me, but I had to admit, she kind of had a point when it came to Roger's *stache*. When we'd been together he'd kept his face clean-shaven for the most part, with the occasional scruff if he got lazy and didn't shave for a few days over the course of a vacation or long weekend.

Roger reached up and brushed the edges of his facial hair. "What's wrong with my mustache?" he asked.

I smiled and hit a few more keys on the register, prompting the printer to spit out another batch of reports. "Nothing, it's fine."

Selene made an undignified gagging sound.

"Hmm." Roger finished smoothing his mustache, then slipped his hands back into the pockets of his well-worn jeans. "All right, so I've grown a mustache, lost my job and fancy condo lease. That sums up how things are going for me. Your turn. What have you been up to?"

"Well, I've been—"

"A whole lot of nothing, that's what she's been up to," Selene interjected. "Do you know what time she went to bed last night? Eight-thirty. Eight. Thirty. She might as well move into a nursing home and spend her nights complaining about the split pea soup."

I cast a withering glare at Selene. *Strike two, kitty cat ...*

"If I go to bed early, it's because I'm pulling four-teen-hour days here at the shop," I said, more for Selene's benefit than Roger's.

"You're still running the place solo?" Roger asked, concern showing along his brow. "Where's Leanna?"

"She got a job working in the admin office at the high school. She needed the benefits, and I couldn't offer them to her. I had a couple of part-timers over the summer, but they were both college students and just left to get back to school, so I'm all alone now."

I winced. I hadn't meant to sound quite so pathetic and lonely.

"Yeah, all alone," Selene piped in. "Except for the men she meets after using those sexy-time dream candles. I tell you what, she's her own best customer—"

"That's it!" I decided then and there it was strike three for Selene the cat. I called up a handful of magic, and conjured a miniature tornado on the counter beside the cat. Selene leaped to her feet and scrambled to flee, all four feet moving like some-thing out of a cartoon, but she failed to make headway against the cyclone. The swirling wind surrounded her, creating a soundproof bubble as her words were sucked into the vortex of wind before they could reach us.

The silence only lasted for a few moments before she fired back with a magic jolt of her own that bought her just enough time to slip free of the wind. She let out a hiss, then scrambled up behind a shelf filled with candelabras. "Ha! You're not the first witch to try and trap me in a tornado. You have to wake up pretty early in the morning to outsmart me, mortal!"

"Do I need to call PETA?" Roger teased, quirking a brow in my direction.

"She's not an animal," I muttered, scowling over my shoulder at the beast, "she's a demon."

"Are you cat sitting or something?"

"No," I rubbed my temples and let out a heavy sigh. "Aunt Lavender went off on one of her quests, leaving Selene behind. She showed up on my doorstep about six weeks ago, and now I'm stuck with her."

"Trust me, if I could break this spell, I'd have gone somewhere—*anywhere*—else," Selene sniped from her cubby. "I have to follow the Hearth family line, from generation to generation, until I die. Which … will be forever, unless those bumbling

Fates manage to figure out where I've hidden my last thread." She flashed a wicked grin.

Roger frowned up at the cat. "You're seriously immortal?"

Selene puffed out her chest. "For all intents and purposes. Cats are gifted with nine lives, but I managed to wrestle my ninth lifeline from the old biddies, and without it, they can't send me packing to the Underworld."

Roger blinked.

"It's a whole thing," I said, dismissing Selene with a wave of my hand. "She's cooked up this story, and it's really best if you don't—"

"Story?" Selene spat. "I'm not making this up! Those hags probably still have scars on their hands from where I scratched them!"

"Yeah, yeah, we get it. You're old. You're vicious. Practically a saber-toothed tiger, yadda, yadda."

Selene narrowed her eyes. "Just for that, I'm ordering *twice* the amount of caviar next week."

"Wow. You've really got a lot going on here, huh?" Roger interjected.

"That's putting it mildly," I replied. "Listen, I have to turn you down on the dinner thing."

"Oh," Roger said, unable to mask the disappointment in his tone.

"But maybe we can get together before you leave," I hastily amended. "I mean, you know, I'm sure we can find some time when our schedules coincide, that sort of thing."

I was well aware of how banal my voice sounded. Roger nodded, then patted his palms on the edge of the front counter before backpedaling a step. "All right, I'll see you later, then." He went to the front door and looked over his shoulder one last time. "It really was good seeing you again, Cora. Take care of yourself."

"You too, okay?"

He smiled and then was gone.

I locked up the store and proceeded to count the till. I bundled up the cash with a rubber band and filled out a deposit slip, leaving aside a hundred dollars in bills and change to keep the register stocked.

"So, what happened between you and the oaf?" Selene asked once I shut the cash drawer. By some miracle she'd finally stopped trying to talk to me when I was in the middle of counting the money.

"I really don't want to talk about it," I replied.

She must have sensed how close I was to blowing a gasket, because she fell silent and let me finish my closing routine in peace. I went about my shop, straightening shelves and doing a casual mental inventory so I knew what I'd need to whip up the following morning before opening. Next, I got the Windex and cleaned the glass cases where I held some of my more elaborately styled candelabras— ones wrought from expensive metals, or bejeweled, or both. I wrinkled my nose in disgust at the many finger smudges. Really, why did everyone have to paw up my display glass?

I got the push broom out and swept the wood floor, then took a long moment to consider whether I should mop or not. Sighing, I decided to give it a go. It wasn't like I had anything else to do. Kayaking was out and the library was already closed. If I went home, I'd likely just veg on the couch with some trashy reality show I didn't even care about. Might as well be productive and save myself some time in the morning. So, I finished mopping and dumped out the water in the utility sink in Wicked Wicks' back of house. I gathered up my bank deposit and hid it inside my purse before turning out the lights and heading for home.

I biked to the bank near the center of town and dropped my deposit in the after-hours slot, before turning around and biking home. My ranch-style house only sat a few blocks away from the center of town, so I biked most days unless it was particularly treacherous in the winter.

I got home and fed Selene, not bothering to banter with the surly cat who was none too pleased with her day-old snapper. I heated up a bowl of leftovers for myself, adding a scoop of rice pilaf and a side salad, and as I sat down in front of the TV, I wondered if maybe Selene was right. Maybe I *was* boring...

I sat and ate my dinner, wondering how differently my night could have gone had Roger not shown up right at the last second to scare off Clint. What would we be doing now? Would the night have ended with a passionate kiss? Or would it have simply been a night of interesting conversation? In any case, it would have beat the heck out of leftovers and a DVR'd episode of *Love Island*.

I guess I'd never find out.

3

*S*ome people liked to start the day with a fresh cup of coffee, or a glass of orange juice. Perhaps a nice breakfast, including cereal, eggs, and toast. Others liked to rise with the sun and go for a three-mile run, or perform yoga stretches, or jump straight into the shower. And then there were the people who liked to simply roll around in bed until the last moment before they absolutely had to get up.

My morning ritual began with having a snarky cat sitting on my chest demanding breakfast. At least, most of the time it did. On the morning of the third day after Clint and Roger visited Wicked Wicks, I awakened to find something else sitting on my chest.

"What's this?" My voice was thick with sleep. I had awakened from a dream where the handsome stranger, Clint, had returned to Wicked Wicks. And no, I didn't burn a special candle before bed. The handsome stranger just seemed to find his way into my dreams on his own.

"Oh, just today's paper," Selene replied, her tone burgeoning with snark. "I'm sure you'll find the headline to be of *particular* interest."

My eyes narrowed. I turned my head to face the cat perched on my bedside table. "What are you up to, Selene?"

"Oh, I'm not up to anything. After all, it's not as if I'm the one who accepts dates from psychotic killers." Selene's tail twitched. "That's more under your *purr*-view, Cora."

"Selene, I literally just woke up, I haven't had my coffee yet, and I don't have enough brain cells coming online to deal with your alleged wit. Just tell me what's going on."

With a *crack* Selene sent the blinds rolling open, blasting me with sunlight. "Read the headline for yourself. It's all quite self-explanatory from there."

I grimaced, putting a hand in front of my face to block the bright sun searing my sleep-bleary eyes. "That was rude!"

"Just check the paper. It should answer all of your questions, and perhaps lead to a great deal more." Selene sat on her haunches, exhibiting feline patience and more than a little sadism, in my opinion. I didn't know what was on the front page of the paper that Selene wanted me to see so badly. I did know that it wasn't going to be anything pleasant.

I unfurled the newspaper—which had a few cat-chewed pages—and stared at the headline. *Winterspell Police investigate brutal homicide.*

I gasped, unable to believe what I read. Crime was exceedingly rare in Winterspell, though not unheard of. I locked up my shop at night, but I didn't have a security system installed because there didn't seem to be a need.

My eyes darted down to the color photo, which really didn't show much. The view outside of a very nice house, practically a manor, with police tape wound across. I normally would have clucked my tongue in sympathy and turned to the crossword puzzle, but Selene's insistence I would find something relevant in the headline made me continue to read.

My gaze fell upon a small rectangular photo beside the headline's text. My lips flew open as a gasp escaped, because there, staring back at me from the paper, was Clint.

Well, that explained why he hadn't been back to my shop. I'd hoped he might wander in for a second try at our date.

"He was murdered?" I asked, my tired eyes not fully reading the article.

"No, you dolt. *He's* the murderer!" Selene scolded me.

"What?"

I read on, and my surprise only grew as the article unfolded. The murder victim was Seth Bridges. He was found by his wife in their home two nights ago, though the police weren't releasing any information on the cause of death. The surprising part was Clint's relation to Seth.

Clint shared the same last name. Clint Bridges. The handsome stranger, the one I'd hit it off with so well, stood accused of murdering his own brother. Or at the least, I realized as I read on, he was a person of interest in the case. Wanted for questioning. Did that mean he'd gone on the run?

No wonder Selene had been so smug and cryptic. The cat had to be loving it, given her penchant for gossip.

"This is just sad, Selene." I folded the paper closed

and rubbed the sleep out of my eyes. "I can't imagine killing my brother."

"You threaten to kill Evan all the time," Selene said. "Last Yuletide, you said, and I quote, 'Evan, I'm going to throttle you if you don't shut up.'"

"He was about to tell Mom about the time I cut school to go skinny dipping with my friends back in high school. That's not appropriate Yuletide conversation. Besides, everyone knew I wasn't seriously going to kill him."

I shook my head and sighed. I never did like violence, starting from a young age. I'd never liked war movies or anything with lots of blood and guts. Even as an adult, my entertainment tastes ranged from reality dating shows to Star Wars and comic book movies, but skipped over things like *Saving Private Ryan*.

Sure, as a teen, enduring my brother's adolescent antics, there were times I would have liked to sock him in the face, but we never did get physical with one another. My family may not have been perfect, but they weren't *that* dysfunctional.

I couldn't imagine life without my brother, let alone the thought of being the one to end his life.

"What a sad story," I said, setting the paper aside before rolling out of bed.

"That's all you have to say about it?" Selene asked, scampering after me as I padded down the hall toward the kitchen. "You almost went on a date with a murderer!"

"First of all, we don't know if he did it," I told her as I stifled a yawn. "He hasn't been arrested."

"Well, what if he did?" she asked.

I shrugged. "It's not like they just found human remains in the guy's basement, Selene. You're making it sound like I narrowly avoided a brush with death."

"We don't know that you didn't!" she insisted.

It was too early for this kind of conversation. As far as I was concerned, it was a family tragedy, and if Clint was in fact a killer, the police would sort it out. In either case, I knew I wouldn't be seeing him again soon. So, what difference did it really make?

Ignoring the cat dancing around my feet, I set up the coffee pot and then went to the fridge and pulled out a tub of the twenty-dollar-a-pound, all natural, chef-prepared, one-hundred-percent organic cat food, which was the only brand the crotchety old cat would eat. A bag of Friskies simply wasn't an option.

After carefully warming the bowl in the microwave and giving it a good stir to avoid any hot spots, I placed the food at Selene's feet. Luckily, she

41

ate her morning meal with gusto and left me alone as I went about my morning routine.

Mostly.

While the coffee finished brewing, I shuffled down the hall to my bathroom. The rising sun caused me to squint as I passed by the east-facing picture window. The spectacular view warmed my heart most mornings, but the homicide in Winterspell cast an intangible pall over my spirits.

I stepped into the shower before it had fully heated up and gasped, throwing a palm up to protect myself from the chill deluge. The cold water snapped me fully into wakefulness. I preferred the water to be very hot, even though my mother told me it would dry out my skin.

When I emerged from the shower amid a cloud of steam, I felt a bit better. Despite my protests to Selene, it did feel somewhat ominous to have been so close to a murder, even if Clint wasn't the one behind his brother's untimely death. I'd never even heard of a murder in Winterspell before, at least not in recent memory.

After dressing, I turned my mind to the day's list of tasks. I'd need to stay late in order to replenish the stock at the shop for the upcoming week. After coffee and a light breakfast, I locked up the house and climbed onto my bike. Selene leaped into the basket hanging from the front, her paws resting on the wicker rim.

"Try not to hit every pothole on the way for a change."

"Don't make me hit a big one on purpose," I muttered.

I pedaled to my shop, trying not to think of Clint, and largely failed until I pulled into the alley behind Wicked Wicks and slowed to a stop beside the metal utility door. While I extracted the keys from my purse, the door adjacent to my own swung open. A ten-inch-tall, pink-haired, iridescent-winged woman flew out, waggling a pink wand adorned with a star shape. The wand emanated a field of glittering pixie dust, which enveloped the twin garbage bags floating in the air behind her.

"Oh, good morning, Cora."

"Good morning, Julia." *Oh, sweet goddess, no! I must get inside before—*

"I'm really glad I ran into you today," the little fairy said in her spritely voice. "I was hoping you'd try my new blend."

I dropped the keys while Selene indulged in a smug snicker. There was no escape now.

Trying to keep from cringing, I grabbed the keys

from the ground and slowly stood back up. "Um, this is made with actual coffee beans this time, right?"

Julia flicked her wand and the heavy sacks of rubbish sailed into the air and plopped neatly inside the dumpster. "Don't worry, it's not kidney bean coffee. I learned my lesson last time."

Julia waved her wand and a steaming mug of coffee appeared out of thin air. "I dried and roasted one hundred percent arabica beans, seasoned with hints of cinnamon and Mexican vanilla. Then I used only pure spring water for the brew, and a rough grind to bring out the boldness of the flavor."

"That … actually sounds pretty good," I said, taking the cup from the air with cautious optimism. I took a careful sip, and then gagged as grit slid down my throat. "Ack! Julia, when's the last time you checked your filter?"

"Filter?" Julia scratched her chin. "Oh, that's right. I knew I was forgetting something."

I handed the cup back to her, which meant depositing it back in the field of pixie dust. "It sounds like you're on the right track."

I finally made it inside the back of my shop, while Selene cackled with laughter.

"Man, you should have seen your face! You were all like 'ack'! I wish I had opposable thumbs so I could operate a cell phone, because that would have gotten soooo many likes on Instagram."

"I'm glad my misery makes you happy," I rasped. I seized on a half-empty bottle of sports drink and guzzled it down. "How does she stay in business with coffee that bad?"

"Overflow," Selene said. "You know, for a businesswoman, you should understand these things. There are exactly two coffee shops in Winterspell, and Dragon's Gold is always crowded."

I swigged down the last of the sports drink and tossed the bottle into the recycling bin under my desk. "At least she stopped trying to sell biscotti."

Selene smiled. "Yeah, I heard a sentry cracked a tooth on the last batch."

I didn't bother counting my till, since I had counted it last night and it looked the same when I opened the cash register. As I often did, I set up a mini workshop on my sales counter. That way, I could create merchandise for restock and special orders while watching the shop.

At nine a.m. sharp, I flipped the sign over to OPEN and turned on the lights. I had my first customer at five past the hour when Mrs. Blanken-ship came in for her usual: a candle that made her husband's cigar smoke turn into the same scent as bakery-fresh cinnamon rolls.

Around ten in the morning, an adolescent witch came in with her parents. She proved fascinated with my candle-making process.

"How do the magical candles work?" The girl's eyes squinted narrow as she watched me pour a stream of melted wax into a clay mold.

"Just like magic scrolls, potions, and infusions. Magic needs a medium to interact with our world. You can use spoken words, syllables, and incantations, or you can use a physical medium."

"Like a candle," the girl said.

"Like a candle." I set the wick carefully, using a long metal strip to adjust the position slightly.

"What kind of candle is that?"

"Well, this is a custom order." I left the mold to cool and solidify and flashed the girl a smile. "It creates an interactive dream if you light it before bed, wherein you're transported to Coney Island."

"Coney Island? Why not Disney World?"

"As I said, it's a custom order, and the customer who buys it used to live in New York. Being able to visit Coney Island in his dreams makes him feel less homesick."

The girl's parents checked out, effectively ending

the demonstration and the conversation in one fell swoop. I returned to creating merchandise, and, between a steady stream of customers and my crafting, the day passed swiftly.

I took a break for lunch, turning my sign to CLOSED and pedaling down to the local deli. I returned to the shop bearing a chicken salad sandwich and cold iced tea.

I had learned long ago that the fastest way to get business through my door was to try to eat. I tackled my sandwich, bite by bite, in between helping customers and occasionally working on my stock.

I was slurping the last remnants of watery tea at the bottom of my cup when I went to lock up for the night. I counted up the day's business and whistled at the stack of bills. I would definitely be making a stop at the bank tonight.

I dragged my bike out the back door, Selene already in the basket, and turned to lock up. I pushed the bike a few feet and looked up to find someone standing in my way.

"Excuse me—" I gasped when I saw who it was.

Clint stood in the alleyway clearly waiting for me.

4

I summoned a whirling dervish of wind in the center of my hand. It was instinctual more than anything, but I kept the swirling mini tornado, just in case. "What are you doing here?" My heart was crammed into my throat, making it a struggle to get the words out. The last thing I had expected was to see Clint in my alleyway.

"I saw the paper this morning," I told him. "Did you really kill your brother?"

Thick brows came low over soulful brown eyes swimming with anxiety. "Of course I didn't kill him."

"That's not what the paper said," Selene interjected.

"Technically the paper said he was a person of interest." I lowered my hand and closed my fist, snuffing out the cyclone. "What are you doing here, Clint?" I asked again.

"I came because I need your help." Clint's shoulders deflated with a sigh as he cast his gaze to the ground between us. "I—I don't really have anywhere else to turn and the police told me not to leave town."

Selene narrowed her eyes. "Hey, buddy, do you see a sign that says 'we smuggle fugitives for a fee'? Get lost."

"Hush, Selene." I considered Clint, noting his haggard appearance. Dark circles lurked under his eyes, and a day's growth of beard stubbled his features. From the looks of his bloodshot eyes and swollen face, he'd done some crying recently. "You really didn't kill your brother?"

"No, I didn't." Clint ran a hand through his hair and shook his head in exasperation. "I told the police as much. I told them everything I know, but they refuse to believe me."

"Why not?" I asked.

"Why are you talking to this crazed, psychotic killer?" Selene's tail twitched back and forth in agitation. "I mean, look at him. He's probably one of those so-called nice guys who sees red and just snaps! Then you'll wish you'd listened to me."

"Selene, be quiet for once." I shifted my gaze back to Clint. "Go on."

Clint hugged himself, suppressing a shudder. "I don't like to think about it, you know? It doesn't even seem real. I just saw Seth on Friday, and now he's gone."

"So you did have contact with him?" I asked.

"Listen to you. I guess you learned something binge watching all those seasons of *Law and Order*."

I ignored Selene as Clint spoke.

"I saw him at our mother's lake house Friday morning. I tried to see him again, later that afternoon, but he was in some kind of meeting." Clint shook his head. "I didn't even see him the second time, I swear, let alone kill him."

"The cops have to be looking at you for more reasons than simple proximity." I swatted away a fly that seemed intent on landing on my face. Despite its wintry name, Winterspell in summer reached temperatures high enough to bead sweat on both our faces. "What aren't you telling me?"

Clint's face twisted into a grimace. Whatever he was about to say, Clint anticipated a bad taste in his mouth afterward.

"I'm not visiting my family in Winterspell just by chance. My mother summoned me here because she wanted to discuss some … changes that she made to her will."

I cocked an eyebrow. "Go on."

Clint sighed, lips becoming a thin, tight line. "She … look, I'm not the marrying kind, all right? I know it's kind of the expected thing, to get married and have a couple of kids, and that's totally fine, for other people. I just don't think that's going to be my life's path."

"I see." I felt a bit disappointed, but then berated myself for it. After all, the man was an accused killer. "What does that have to do with your mother's will?"

Clint's lips twisted in the ghost of a mirthless, sardonic smile. "My mother had originally wished to split the inheritance evenly between her two sons. However, when I told her that I wasn't going to start a family, she decided I didn't need as big a cut of the family estate. She changed the will so my brother Seth would be inheriting the bulk of her wealth."

The grin grew somewhat genuine. "After all, he's already started his family. Or I should say, he had started …"

Clint looked as if he were battling a renewed wave of tears. He scrubbed a hand down his face before he continued speaking. "Anyway, the police see that—the money, I mean—as plenty of motive for murder. That's why I'm the prime suspect. Oh, wait, I'm sorry. Person of interest."

I felt sympathy blossom in my chest, in spite of the fact I didn't know Clint all that well. It didn't mean I still wasn't wary of him. After all, I had literally just met the man.

"Look, Clint, I'm not sure what you think I can do for you. I don't even know a good lawyer. I really can't get tangled up in this kind of thing, okay?"

"Tangled up?" Clint's brows lifted. "What are you talking about?"

"Look, I'm a business owner, all right? My clientele is my lifeblood. My reputation directly affects how many people walk through the front door and buy candles."

"Cora, I don't think you—"

I shook my head. "No can do. I think your best bet is to speak with an attorney and let them hash it out with the police."

Clint looked increasingly anxious. He fidgeted, pacing about in the alley as he spoke. "That's just the thing, though. I *have* contacted my lawyer. He's coming, he's on his way, but in the meantime, I need to borrow a computer. That's why I came here, I thought you might be kind enough to let me use yours."

I was taken aback by the strange request. "A computer? You're walking around in a Hugo Boss suit and you don't have a computer, or a tablet? Anything at all?"

I eyed Clint with suspicion, a fact that was not lost on him. "The cops confiscated my laptop as evidence, all right? I'm not making up an excuse just to trick you."

"What about a tablet?"

"I had an iPad, and they took that, too."

"Cell phone?"

"Confiscated."

I heaved a long sigh.

Clint held up a hand. "Look, I've been negotiating a huge business deal for some time, and right now it's balanced very precariously. If I don't check in with my potential new client soon, they're going to give up on me. Period, end of story." He gestured helplessly. "They took everything I had, every means of getting online. So unless there's an internet café in town, I'm kind of at your mercy. My mother wants nothing to do with me right now. She has my brother's wife … or, widow, I suppose, at the house and she's bought into the police's theory."

"The gas station down the way sells those pay-as-you-go phones," I told him.

"A burner phone?" Clint shook his head in disgusted vehemence. "One simply does not conduct multimillion-dollar business deals on a burner phone. And it's not like there's an Apple store or Best Buy in Winterspell."

"I guess most of us rely on magic more than technology." I shrugged. "The younger citizens are more into tech, but they drive into one of the bigger towns to get it."

"Well, driving anywhere outside of city limits isn't an option for me any longer." Clint sighed. "Please, I promise I won't take up much of your time. All I want to do is get back to my hotel room. Now that my face has been splashed all over the local paper, I'm getting a little too much attention out and about."

I hesitated while clutching the bars of my bike with a white-knuckled grip. I hated to turn away someone in need, but at the same time, I really didn't want to get mired in the tangle of a murder investigation. What if the police found out I let him use my computer? Would that cast some suspicion on me? I suppose I could lie, say I hadn't seen the paper. Of course, Selene would probably rat me out if an officer so much as hinted at getting her a reward.

In the end, my basic human decency won out, but it was a close call. "All right."

"Great, here we go. Now we're going to get robbed and wrapped up with duct tape, just like on that episode of *NCIS*."

"Be quiet, Selene," I gasped.

"Do I really look threatening?" Clint asked, with a slight scoff to the question. "I don't even know how to use my own magic beyond a few party tricks. If anything, Cora is a threat to me."

"I'm not a threat to anyone," I said, unlocking the back door and allowing Clint inside. I decided to leave my bike sitting in the alley. No one was likely to steal it in Winterspell.

Then again, I had thought the same about murder until this morning.

I led him through the back area to my front of house. I puttered around the shop looking for my laptop while Clint perused my wares.

"You know, it would really simplify things if you sold me a candle that would convince the cops I was telling the truth." He lifted up a wrapped blueberry-colored candle and idly examined it before setting it down. "Say, weren't you telling me about some kind of lie detector candle?"

"What?" I paused as my fingers finally brushed

the smooth case of my computer. It had been hiding in a drawer under my cash register. "I said no such thing."

"I could have sworn you did." Clint searched carefully through my merchandise until he came up with a candle the color of Selene's eyes. "Here it is right here. Heart's Truth."

"That candle isn't a lie detector, Clint," I replied dryly. "I said that it would cause a person to reveal their true desires. It's more of a decision-making tool. It reveals what you want, not what you've done."

"Can you give me an example?"

"Well, it won't make someone blurt out that they're having an affair or stole the crown jewels or anything like that. It's more ..." my hand gestured in the air, as if trying to grasp the right words. "More like, if someone's always wanted to be a painter, or learn to dance ballet, or to climb Mount Everest. That sort of thing."

"I see," Clint said, shoulders slumping in defeat.

I sighed. "I'm sorry. I've never heard of magic that would work that way. If there were, the police would have access to it, not me."

"Right. Of course." Clint shook his head, as

though chiding himself for even asking in the first place.

Selene leaped up onto the counter and stared meaningfully at me. "Once again, you insult me, Cora!"

"What? How have I insulted you?"

Selene turned toward Clint, her tail twitching in annoyance. "You told Mr. Ripper that you couldn't help him without even consulting me."

"Wait, your cat knows more about magic than you do?" Clint sounded incredulous.

"Oh, don't sound so suspicious, you hairless ape. I'm the oldest and wisest sentient being in this here candle shop."

"Selene does have a ton of magical knowledge," I said slowly. Then my eyes narrowed. "But she never, ever gives anything away for free. There's always a price, isn't there, Selene?"

"I'll pay any price," Clint said eagerly. "I'll do anything you want if you'll help me."

"Anything?" Selene's blue eyes glittered with pure, unadulterated greed.

"Selene, don't you dare shake him down just because he's desperate—"

My voice trailed off as I glanced out the window

and saw a police cruiser pulling up outside my shop, lights flashing. "Oh no …"

In a panic, I grabbed Clint's arm and shoved him toward the back room. "Go! Get moving!"

I relentlessly shooed him off the sales floor and into the back of house. I kept pushing until we were in a small storage room, out of sight of the front windows of my shop. "Now stay."

A knock at the door nearly caused me to jump out of my skin. Heart pounding, I held a finger to my lips and then turned away from Clint.

I crept back to the open doorway separating the stockroom from the sales floor and peered carefully out.

A uniformed police officer stood at the front door of the shop. As I watched, he raised his hand and rapped on my door with his knuckles. A very insistent rapping at that.

"Well, Cora," Selene said "I guess you had a pretty good run, but this is it. Aiding and abetting a fugitive? Aww, man! Better start learning to carve a shiv and getting used to the idea of eating tater tots and fish sticks for the next ten to twenty."

I was too frightened to be angry at my ancient familiar.

What have I got myself into this time?

5

I wrestled with myself, poised at the edge of the archway separating the stockroom from the sales floor. Beyond the rows of shelves filled with candles, I could see the police officer peering through the sheer curtain hung in the plate glass window, hand cupped to reduce the glare of the setting sun.

"Well? No use in putting off the inevitable." Selene's ears twitched back. "No worries, I'm sure you can pick up another degree or two while you're in the big house."

"What even makes you think that I'm going away to prison? I took Clint in on good faith." My eyes narrowed. "Answer me that, Miss Smarty Pants."

"Miss Smarty Pants? Are we pulling the preschool-level ordnance from our insult arsenal?"

"We don't even know he's here for Clint," I fired back. "And he wasn't arrested, remember? So, I'm hardly aiding and abetting."

"Unless Clint lied," Selene countered. "And let's be honest, your taste in men is questionable at best. It wouldn't really be a surprise to find you've fallen for a pathological liar, would it?"

I ground my teeth.

Selene leaned in. "If the cop wasn't here for Clint, then why did he have his lights flashing when he pulled up? Hmm?"

I didn't have an answer for that.

"Yeah, that's what I thought. Face it. Shake down, take down … you're busted."

"What?" I tilted my head to the side. "What's that even from?"

"*Beverly Hills Cop.*"

"Oh, I don't think I was even born when that came out."

"So now we're being ageist?"

I put a finger to her nose. "Quiet. Let me go see what he wants."

I took a deep breath, held it for four seconds like my mother had taught me, and then let it out slowly through my nostrils. I opened my eyes, and felt my heart rate had decreased at least a little bit.

Steeling myself, I strode out of the back room confidently toward the front door. At least, I hoped I looked confident, and not like someone about to break under the pressure of accidentally harboring a maybe-fugitive.

I noticed he'd turned his lights off, so I had that much to be grateful for, at least. I took one final, calming breath, and opened the door. "Can I help you?"

"Sorry to bother you after business hours, ma'am." The thirtyish deputy spoke politely, but his eyes seemed hard and suspicious to my estimation. "I see you're closed up for the evening, but do you have time to answer a few questions?"

"Questions? About what?" I winced inwardly at the banality of my own voice. Surely the cop would see right through my innocent act.

"Perhaps we could discuss this inside?" The officer peered behind me into the gloom of the darkened candle shop.

The last thing I wanted was to let the deputy inside my shop with Clint there. Yet, I feared it would make me look suspicious to refuse him entry. I eventually decided to let him in, and prayed to all of the goddesses that Clint was good at keeping quiet.

"Certainly." I stepped back from the door and allowed the deputy inside. I swiftly retreated behind the sales counter, as if the physical barrier could somehow protect me from suspicion as well. The deputy clumped across the polished hardwood floor to stand before the counter. "Now what can I help you with, officer?"

He stared at me for a long, agonizing moment before his brow furrowed in query. "Do you recall selling a silver candelabra and an assortment of candles to a customer on Thursday afternoon?"

My knees buckled. There was exactly one and only one person who'd purchased those items in that combination. Clint. I decided it would do me no good to lie. "It was a pretty busy afternoon, but yes, I remember selling a gift basket that fits that description. Can I ask what this is about?"

The deputy didn't answer my question, but instead asked another one of his own. "Can you describe the customer to me?"

"Um, early thirties, Caucasian male," my voice broke awkwardly. "Dark brown hair, kind of on the slender side. Wore a nice suit, if I recall."

The deputy took out a notepad and scribbled on

the surface. "Did the customer happen to give his name?"

"Um, Clint, I think."

The deputy didn't make a sound, but his eyes shone with an eager light. He scribbled on his notepad furiously. I got the impression of a big hound dog who'd just hit upon a tasty scent. "How did this Clint pay for his purchase?"

"He used a credit card."

"Could I get a copy of the receipt?"

I nodded, wanting to fall over in relief. He hadn't come because he thought I was harboring a fugitive, despite his dramatic entrance with the lights flashing and all. He was just checking into a lead, which unfortunately would lead him right to the man cowering in my supply room.

I took out my tablet and tapped the screen to life. I flipped through the receipts, organizing them by time to make the task faster. I found the receipt in question and hit the print icon. The laser printer under the register came to life, quickly spitting out a receipt.

"Here you go." My hand shook slightly as I handed off the copy. The deputy glanced at it and nodded.

"Thanks a lot." He carefully folded the receipt in

half, leaving a crisp edge of razor perfection, and stuffed it into an envelope. "I appreciate your cooperation in not making me get a warrant for this."

I shrugged. "There's exactly one enchanted candle shop in town. What would the point be of obfuscating where the gift basket came from?"

The man's brows climbed his forehead. "You'd be surprised, ma'am."

"I'm sure I would be." I swallowed, hard. "Um, is this about the case in the paper this morning? The man who killed his own brother?"

"I'm really not supposed to comment on an ongoing investigation ..." the deputy said, pursing his lips. I started to open my mouth to say I understood when he continued. "But, seeing as you've been so cooperative and all, and in a town this small it'll be all over the place in a couple days anyway ... there were witnesses who put Clint outside the victim's house on the night of the murder. Not to mention his fingerprints all over the candelabra that was used as the murder weapon."

I flinched. I hadn't known that the murder weapon was an item I had sold in my own shop. That thought gave me a very creepy feeling.

"Wow" was all I was able to say.

The deputy's eyes dawned with a sudden realization. "Oh, there was something else I'd like to ask you about."

"What's that?" I frowned as he opened his folder and extricated a color photo. He turned it around so I could see it.

"This candle was found burned to the wick on the victim's desk. Did it come from your shop?"

My heart sank as I examined the photo and saw the blackened, curled petals of a wildflower in the pool of melted wax. "That looks like one of mine, all right. Why?"

"Well, the wax was still in a liquid state when we arrived on scene. How long does a candle like that last?"

"About four to five hours, give or take." I shook my head as I examined the photo. "But that number can vary quite a bit based on things like ambient temperature, ventilation, and such."

"So, what would a candle like this do while it was lit?"

"I'm sorry?"

"What kind of magical effect does it produce?"

I blinked in realization. "Oh. Well, that's a tranquility candle. It produces a six-tier illusory field that creates the impression of being in a starlit meadow."

"Six-tier illusory field?" He shook his head. "I don't have much time to study illusion magic. It's mostly wards and defenses for us deputies."

"Sorry, officer. Didn't mean to make myself sound all hoity-toity. The illusion is six-tier because it affects all five of the physical senses, plus creates a mental illusion as well."

"Why the mental illusion?"

"Because of immersion. It leads to a more cohesive fantasy, plus they're designed with anyone in mind, including those who may have lost their sight or hearing."

"Fascinating." He took some more notes on his pad. "So, how does one break out of the illusion?"

"You can blow out the candle or wait for it to sputter out when the wick is spent. That ends the effect for everyone involved."

"Could someone have, say, been under the influence of your candle, and seen Seth as a threat?" The cop tapped his pen on his notepad, eyes wide and expectant.

I was taken aback by the question. It sounded almost accusatory. "Why, no. No! There's no way. That's not how the illusion works. It only alters your perception of the environment, not any living creatures in the area of effect."

The deputy nodded and scribbled down a note. "I see."

I cleared my throat. I tended to drone on when speaking about my candles. "None of my products can cause any harm, officer. I promise you that."

"From what we could tell, your candle didn't do a bit of harm." He snapped his notepad closed and stuffed it in his front pocket. With a click of his pen, he nodded politely at me. "It was the candelabra that did our victim in."

He turned to leave, but I had one final question. "Oh, officer?"

The deputy paused halfway to the door. "Yes, ma'am?"

"When you pulled up outside my shop, you had your lights flashing. I was just wondering why you had them on."

The deputy eyes widened. "Oh, that. Well, it's summer, you know? A lot of tourists in town, and some of them have bored kids. I saw a couple of teens with a can of spray paint by your side wall. I flashed my lights to scare them off, but you might want to check and see if they left you any 'presents.'"

"Oh. Thanks, I guess."

He nodded and pushed his way out the front door.

I felt my stomach bottom out. I gripped the edge of the counter, trying to will the nausea away as the deputy took his leave. As soon as the door closed behind him, I summoned up two cyclones, one in each palm, and rushed into the stock area.

"Clint!" I snapped. "You never said anything about being at Seth's house around the time of the murder, or that the candelabra I sold you wound up being the murder weapon!"

No response. I moved fully into the back of house area but found no answers forthcoming from the bare drywall and finished concrete floors. "Clint? Hello?"

I grew wary and summoned my magic once again. "Clint, are you in here? The cop is gone, and he wasn't even after you. Sorry I flipped out and shoved you back here like a tawdry secret."

I still received no response. My face contorted into a scowl. "This isn't funny! Come out, already."

I moved into the last corner of the stock room and found nothing, no sign of Clint. I leaned on a shelf and frowned, trying to figure out what could have happened to him.

"Where the heck did he go?"

"Are you talking about Clint?" Selene asked with grating innocence as she padded up.

"No, I'm talking about the Mad Hatter. Of course I mean Clint! Where did he get off to? He was just here."

"Oh, I don't think he stuck around long after that cop showed up." Selene was enjoying every moment of the game. I tried not to let on how frustrated I was. If Selene figured out that her antics were getting to me in any way, it would only prolong the agony.

"Selene," I said, with exaggerated calmness and a casual tone. "Did you happen to see what happened to Clint?"

"Why yes, yes I did." Selene licked her paw, eyes half lidded.

I fought down a nasty retort. "Can you tell me where he went, please?"

"Of course I can." Selene looked at me for a long moment as if I were quite dumb and went back to the bath.

"Then tell me, please," I said through gritted teeth.

"He headed out the back right when the cop came."

"I guess he was worried …" I cocked an eyebrow at Selene. The little cat seemed quite smug about something. "There's something you're not telling me."

"Oh, I haven't even gotten to the good part." Her tail swished with excitement. "He took your laptop with him."

"He what?" My voice went up an octave. "He stole my laptop?"

"Well, these things happen when you harbor fugitives from justice."

"Will you knock it off?" I shook my head. "Selene, why didn't you try to stop him when you saw him stealing my laptop?"

The cat's eyes narrowed. "Excuse me?"

Selene calmly licked her front paw, then peered up at me. "What do I look like, your mangy guard dog?"

"No," I growled. "But maybe I should look into getting one of those. They might be the only thing that could keep you in line."

$\mathcal{I}$ don't know what made me madder. The fact that Clint had stolen my laptop, or the way that Selene made sure to rub it in. She spent the whole night making passive-aggressive statements to me about the whole affair.

"Hey, can you get me the routing number for your account—oh, that's right. You're out of checks but you have a picture saved on the laptop. Where did that get off to again?"

Or, "I'll bet you'd like to look at your sales invoices for last quarter. Too bad they're on the laptop. When's Clint supposed to get that back to you again?"

And my personal favorite, "You don't suppose Clint is going to download some government secrets or something onto your hard drive do you? Wouldn't that be so incriminating? But I'm sure he's a trustworthy sort, I mean, accused of murder and all."

It was enough to get me thinking about conjuring up a windstorm and putting her through her own personal spin-cycle like in a washing machine, but I managed to tamp that idea down, had a glass of wine, and went to bed.

The next day, I closed up shop early because I had book club. Generally speaking, I wasn't a huge fan of book club, but it was one of the few purely social things I did in Winterspell. Plus, it was a chance to catch up with my friend Leanna. I missed her since she took a job at the school and left Wicked Wicks.

The host of book club is a woman I went to high school with, Judy Grimm. She's a fire witch, but not much of a caster. She chose not to go on to university and instead married young to start a family. Judy's all right, but she's a housewife with two maids and a personal chef. All that free time leads to her favorite hobby: gossiping, and stars above is she good at it.

Mainly, I just go to see Leanna, but there's some other folks in the "sort of acquaintance" category I hang out with, too. Most of the time, I couldn't care less about what book we're talking about.

I do care about the snacks. That personal chef I mentioned? Yeah, it turns out she studied abroad, and is nothing short of amazing. You never know what you're going to come across when you show up at book club. One week there were these crab cakes with a flambée crust that just melted in our mouths. Then on another occasion we were treated to cucumber sandwiches, which may not sound good but trust me: it was one of the best things I've ever eaten. Creamy and cool and everything you could ask for on a hot summer's day.

The snacks alone would be enough to keep me coming back, but then they go on ahead and tempt you with wine. Not just any wine, either. I'm talking stuff that wins international awards, always perfectly paired with the snacks. That's one thing I'll give Judy: she doesn't skimp on book club night.

I pulled up in front of the Grimms' residence, a three-story contemporary home with a back yard big enough to fit my house, the entirety of Wicked Wicks, and my garage with room to spare.

A blue Toyota Camry nimbly dodged into the parking spot just ahead of mine as I turned off the engine. A smile broke out on my face when I recognized the vehicle, and its driver. Leanna and I got out of our respective vehicles at roughly the same time.

"Hey, you." I walked toward her, and we embraced. Leanna is one of the sweetest, least jaded people I know. Normally when you hear someone described as "bubbly" it's a veiled code for annoying or over the top. Not with Leanna. I can't imagine her any other way, nor would I want to.

We were both dressed up a little for the occasion, each wearing a strappy sundress and sandals. Leanna's umber skin always made bright colors pop, and it was no exception with the jewel-toned purple dress she wore tonight.

"How are you?" I asked as we parted from the embrace.

She brushed her long, curly hair out of her honey-brown eyes and shrugged. "Same stuff, different day," she replied. "I was actually wondering if you'd like to come in and speak to a group of freshmen."

"Me? Why?" I shook my head. "I'm not good at public speaking."

"You're a female business owner, and a role model. Come on, it could be fun!"

"I'll think about it."

Leanna laughed. "You know I'll just keep hounding you about it, right?"

We turned toward the sidewalk. Judy's house featured a natural hued stone walk. The surface was smooth enough for easy striding and rough enough to show the stone's natural state. Shrubbery sprouted up at intervals along the walk, which opened up into a courtyard area in front of the home's main entrance.

"So, did you hear?" Leanna asked. Though she hadn't provided context, I had no trouble knowing she was talking about the murder investigation.

"Yes, I did. So tragic." My face scrunched up in anger because thinking of the murder made me think of Clint, which made me think of my laptop. I hadn't filed a police report—though I wasn't sure why not. It was on my list of things to do the coming weekend.

"Isn't it, though? Just when you think you're safe …"

"Say, do you remember what we were supposed to read for book club this week?"

"Oh, sweet goddess …" Leanna clapped a hand to her head and sighed. "What was it? *Gone Girl*?"

"Oh lord, I fell asleep during the movie," I

groaned. "Whoever decided that Ben Affleck could act?"

Leanna laughed. "I remember thinking he was cute, back when we were in high school, but the kids now just make memes about how goddess-awful he was as Batman."

We shared a laugh as we reached the front door. I rang the doorbell and then stood back to wait. After several moments Leanna and I exchanged glances. "That's weird."

"Are we supposed to just go in?"

"I don't know. Usually the maid answers by now—"

The door popped open and a middle-aged woman in simple gray garments nodded in greeting. "Welcome. Mrs. Grimm is on the patio."

"The patio?" Leanna frowned. "That's kind of strange. We almost never have book club on the patio."

Leanna and I followed the maid through the gallery and down a short hallway to the kitchen. My mouth watered at the sight of all the delectable treats arrayed on neat trays upon the marble countertops. It looked as if no one had even partaken of the snacks yet.

My confusion grew when we reached the back

patio and found everyone clustered around one woman, someone I'd only met in passing before. I couldn't recall her name, but I felt as if I should.

The woman was visibly pregnant and cradled her stomach as she sat in a patio chair. Her face glistened with tears as she spoke in garbled sentences I couldn't fully make out. Whatever she was saying, she had the ear of every other member of the club as they swarmed around her, offering tissues and words spoken in low, comforting tones.

Thankfully, though the snacks remained inside in the kitchen, the wine was available. Leanna and I each took a glass and sidled up to Heather Barton, another woman I went to school with and one of my aforementioned acquaintances.

"Heather, what's going on? Who is that?" Leanna asked in a whisper.

Heather's lips quivered. "Oh, it's terrible. That's Melissa Bridges. Her husband was murdered yesterday. It's just so awful."

My eyes nearly bugged out of my head, and I choked on my wine. Heather mistook my reaction and bobbled her head in sympathy. "I know, I know. Awful, right?"

I nodded, taking a drink of water to clear my

throat. I listened more intently to what Melissa was saying.

"... I mean, he was just there, laying on the floor. At first I thought he was playing a prank ..." Melissa broke down while the women of book club consoled her. "I—just still can't believe he's really gone!"

"And it was the brother?" Judy asked.

Melissa turned her tear-streaked face toward our hostess and nodded. "Clint. I just don't understand what would make someone do something so awful. I mean, I was trying to get Seth and Clint on better terms again ..."

"They were estranged?" I found myself asking. Clint hadn't mentioned that part either.

Melissa nodded, then wetly blew her nose on a tissue. "I really wanted to bridge the gap between them, you know? I mean, I'm sure that Clint was mad about the will and all, but I had Seth mostly convinced to hand over a good portion of his inheritance anyway, no matter what the will said."

Nods went up around the book club. "I'm sure you did your best, Melissa."

She blew her nose again and took a long drink of wine. "That's it, girl. Drink some more wine, it will help."

Another woman asked if she wanted anything

from the kitchen, but Melissa's face screwed up in misery and she began crying again. "I keep thinking, what if I'd just stayed home that night? What if I'd been there? Then none of this—none of this would have happened."

After that, she broke down into shoulder-shaking sobs. Several of the women told her she couldn't have known, and urged her not to go there. My heart welled with sympathy for her, but I also couldn't resist trying to pry a little more information out of her.

"Melissa can you think of anyone else who might have wanted to hurt your husband? Someone besides his brother?"

Melissa shook her head and sobbed harder. I got dirty looks from just about every pair of eyes at book club, not including Leanna. Although even she had this "what's wrong with you?" look in her eyes.

When we showed up, Melissa's sobbing fit had put that week's book club meeting on life support. Then, when I asked my somewhat insensitive, but sagacious question, I pulled the plug on it and eulogized it. Everyone dispersed, though I did make sure to grab a couple of crab cakes for the road.

Leanna and I made our way down the sidewalk,

heading for the street. She gave me a quizzical look. "What was all of that about?"

"As it turns out, Melissa's brother-in-law stopped off in my shop the day before the murder."

Leanna paused mid-stride. "Okay, hold up. What?"

"He said he was in town to visit his mom, and he wanted to purchase a gift for her. I sold him a really expensive gift basket, and somehow in the process of it all, well he, uh, he asked me to dinner with him."

"Shut up!" Leanna's eyes were wide as dinner plates. "Did you say yes?"

"I didn't have a chance to say anything because Roger turned up right about then, and he asked me to dinner, too."

Leanna laughed and nibbled on the crab cake she held wrapped in a cocktail napkin. "Girl, you have just got to have the worst luck in all of Winterspell. I still can't believe Roger is back in town."

"Tell me about it," I groaned. "Anyway, last night, Clint showed up again, this time asking to use my computer. Then this officer showed up, so I told him to hide, and well … long story short, he stole my laptop."

"This just keeps getting more and more screwed up," Leanna said with a sympathetic shake of her head. "Although, I do want to circle back to the part where you were about to go on a date for the first time in *months* and didn't tell me."

I rolled my eyes as I smiled. "I was a little busy telling you about the Roger thing. It seemed the more pressing of the two events. It's not every day your ex-husband shows up and asks you to dinner."

"Thank the goddess," Leanna muttered.

We joined the general exodus heading for the cars parked along the street. A woman named Sissy —AKA the book club's number one gossip bunny— hustled up to us, her eyes shining with barely contained delight.

"Here we go," I whispered to Leanna, who giggled.

"Can you believe it? A murder in our town?"

"It really is ghastly," I said, trying to get around her so I could reach my car and escape. Without missing a beat, she stepped to the side and blocked my path.

"Well, I would never say this in front of poor Melissa, but if you ask me, she's better off without that Seth."

"What an awful thing to say!" Leanna gasped.

"I'm sorry, but it's true!" Sissy insisted before looking about as if worried we were being eavesdropped upon. The truth was, the rest of our book club now saw Leanna and me as the wounded gazelles, and were using the opportunity to slink away and escape while the lioness was busy.

Sissy leaned in and whispered. "He's been spotted cavorting around town with a bartender at Merlin's Well."

"Cavorting?" I asked.

"Well, that's the polite term for it," Sissy said, her penciled-on eyebrows waggling. "I mean, the man's wife was pregnant and he cheats on her with some piece of fluff serving Fuzzy Navels and draft beer? The shame." She winked at us. "But you didn't hear that from me. Ta-ta!"

I heaved a sigh of relief. The ordeal was over.

I drove back home and relayed the information to Selene. She listened with surprising patience, her blue eyes rapt with attention.

As my story wound down, Selene piped in at last. "You know, I wasn't just trying to wheedle something out of you when I told that Clint fellow I know a spell that can tell us the truth of what happened to his brother."

I cocked an eyebrow at her. "So tell me."

"What's it worth to you?"

I rolled my eyes and sighed. "You're a familiar. It's

your job to be helpful. So, maybe one of these days you could actually try, oh I don't know, *helping*."

"I'm more than willing to be helpful … for a price."

I heaved a sigh. "Good night, Selene."

"When you change your mind, you know where to find me."

I ignored her and trundled off to bed and, hopefully, slumber.

7

*D*awn broke behind gray skies, stifling Winterspell with humidity but refusing to give up a payload of cooling rain. The muggy air hit my face as soon as I opened the front door and I grimaced as I rolled my bike down the short flight of porch steps onto the sidewalk.

"The air is sticky," Selene said with distaste. "We should take the car."

"It's only three blocks, that's just silly."

"Fine, but it's your funeral."

I quickly learned that the cat was right. About a block's worth of pedaling, even taking my time, resulted in my clothes plastered to my body with a layer of sweat. By the time I reached the shop, I was blinking the sweat out of my eyes and feeling like I needed a second shower.

"Ugh, where is autumn when you need it?" I muttered to myself as I summoned up a wind to air-dry after running a cold cloth over my face, neck, and arms. "Seems like we're overdue for some rain."

"You'd think the city council could get off their lazy rear ends and get some water witches on the case," Selene groused from her place on the front counter.

"Yeah, I don't think it works like that," I told her as I began setting out my candle-making supplies.

Selene glared up at me. "Oh, now *you're* going to tell *me* how magic works? Ha! Imagine the gall."

At some point during the morning Selene slipped out the shop's propped-open back door, something she did quite often. I knew better than to worry. Selene was more than capable of handling herself. If anything, it was the rest of Winterspell I should be concerned about.

As I unwound a length of wick from a large spool, a woman approached the counter, her eyes filled with trepidation.

"Hi, can I help you?"

"I hear you do custom orders," she said, voice

breaking. I got the impression whatever her request was, it embarrassed her more than a little.

"I do," I said cautiously. *Please don't let this be something weird ...*

"Could you make one that ..." she lowered her voice and leaned forward over the counter "... one that gave you the impression you were a sloth hanging from a tree over the Congo?"

"Oh," I said, relieved if a little bit confused. "Why, I imagine that I can help you with that, yes. Is there anything specific you want from the experience?"

She shook her head. "Just the ability to hang around in a tree and sleep all day with nobody to bother me is more than enough."

I took out my special request form, a small tablet about half the size of a notebook, and tore off the top sheet before handing it to her. "Just fill this out, please, and check the box next to the size of the candle you want."

"Size matters?"

"The bigger the candle, the longer it lasts," I said with a chuckle.

She wandered off to fill out the form while I went through my stack of unfulfilled custom order requests. Ever since *Bridgerton* got popular I'd been dealing with a lot of costume period piece requests.

It had gotten to the point where I considered adding it to my regular shelf stock.

I worked my way through a couple of custom orders, then went back to making my best seller, the relaxation candle. It seemed like stress was not in short supply in our fair town of Winterspell.

The woman finished her request sheet and was a bit disappointed when I told her it would take three days to complete. She put down a deposit worth ten percent of the total, as is my policy, and took her leave.

I fielded another weird request, this one from a man who wanted the experience of watching a Road Runner/Wile E. Coyote cartoon where the Coyote actually wins. It's not even the weirdest request I'd had that week, but it stood out in my mind for some reason.

One thing about being busy: the day goes by fast. A growling belly spurred me to check and see if it was time for lunch—noonish—and I was shocked to see it was a quarter past three. I went through a recovery on my shop—retailer jargon for straightening up after a rush—and hastened to get through at least a few more custom orders. I didn't want to make the sloth lady wait any longer for her candle than I had told her.

As I carefully pried apart the mold of a Meadow's Eve candle, Selene came slinking back into the shop and went straight to the glass water bowl I kept for her.

After a drink, she leaped up onto the counter, her blue eyes intent. "Hey. Whatcha doing?"

She batted at a tiny pair of pliers until they went over the edge of the counter and clattered to the floor. "Oopsies!" she said with a laugh.

"Selene, where have you been?" I bent over and picked up the pliers. "You've been gone for hours."

"I stopped by Lavender's place to say hey—"

"You mean to roll around in her catnip plants. You're high!"

The cat twitched her whiskers, but didn't bother denying my observation.

"Oh, lighten up!" she finally quipped, before getting distracted by a tiny reflection bouncing off my watch onto the wall behind me. "Ooh! Cora, look!"

I honestly wasn't sure which version of her I liked better. At least when she was high on catnip she wasn't nagging or insulting me.

"The place is looking rough," Selene continued, her gaze still following the shiny spot on the wall. "She's still not back from her trip. The shades are drawn, yard's overgrown. Her mail slot is over-flowing."

My brow furrowed with concern. "You don't think something happened to her, do you?"

"Lavender? Nah." Selene stretched out her spine, flattening out until her belly brushed the counter. "She's probably just off on one of her excursions. You know, trying to find a hidden pyramid in the South American jungle, or trying to uncover Amelia Earhart's plane to prove her theory that the poor dear was a time witch. That sort of thing."

"Yes, but from what you said she's been gone for well over a month now. It seems like we should maybe do something, at some point. Right?"

"Ha! When I was Lavender's familiar, we went on a three-month excursion through the Scottish High-lands looking for some enchanted rock formation," Selene said. "Personally, I think she just fell asleep after watching one too many episodes of Outlander and dreamed the whole thing up. In any case, your aunt can take care of herself. She's been doing it since before you were born."

"Right, but back then she had you," I pointed out, keeping my tone gentle.

The circumstances under which Selene came to be my familiar were something of a sore spot with the cat. Not that I could blame her. As she aged, Aunt Lavender grew more eccentric and flightier. So long as I'd known her, she'd always been one of those "head in the clouds" type of people, but it had grown worse over time. She started forgetting to take Selene with her on her trips, and the cat suffered.

It wasn't a case of a pet missing their owner. With Selene, there is a magical component to her companionship. Something deeper than a guardian and their beloved animal. When Lavender left Selene behind, Selene's own magical lifeblood began to weaken and drain away, leaving her almost completely paralyzed by weakness. At her advanced age, magic was essentially all that was holding her together—well, that and this so-called ninth life she always yammered on about, though I'm pretty sure that's all just a tall tale.

In any case, insufferable though she may be, Selene didn't deserve to slowly waste away, waiting for Lavender's return, so when she'd shown up on my doorstep six weeks ago and explained all of this to me, I'd had no choice but to agree to take her as my own familiar. I wasn't sure how my Aunt Lavender would take the news once she returned to

Winterspell, but I hoped she would understand and not be upset with either Selene or me.

"She'll be fine. Don't be such a worrywart," Selene said, her tone a little snappy. "Heck, I'm on my last life and I've still got more cojones than most of this town."

"You never had cojones ... never mind," I sighed and rubbed my temples. "You really think Aunt Lavender is okay?"

Selene canted her head, still watching the reflection bouncing off my watch. "Of course, the city might not be too happy with her right now, considering all the notices on her porch."

"The city left notices on her porch?"

"Yeah, about trimming her grass and such. I don't blame them, either. Her yard has practically become a jungle. Good hunting grounds for me, but I imagine the neighbors aren't too fond of it."

"This is why I hate Bermuda grass. It's a weed." I sighed. "I'll bring it up at dinner tonight."

"Oh, that's right. Dinner at your mother's place. Do you suppose she's making salmon patties?"

"I don't know what she's making, Selene. Do you want me to ask?"

"Of course not, don't trouble her."

I put my hands on my hips and stared at the gray

cat. "Selene, we go through this every time. You ask if it's going to be salmon patties, I offer to call Mom and ask, and you tell me not to bother. Then, when we actually sit down to eat and it's *not* salmon patties, you sulk and ruin everyone's good time."

"Well, maybe I want your mother to *want* to make salmon patties for me, did you ever consider that? Humph! I've protected and served witches of multiple generations of your family. One might think a little bit of gratitude is in order."

I went back to work, but I managed to sneak out a text asking Mom to please, pretty please with sugar on top make some freaking salmon patties. For everyone's sake.

When it was about ten minutes to closing time, I got a text from Mom. A thumbs-up. She still doesn't have a smartphone, making do with her old flip model. Like many of Winterspell's older residents, she prefers magic to technology. Of course, my mother tends to adopt that policy in the extreme. She has a huge vegetable garden that dominates most of her backyard. She makes her own apple cider vinegar in a tree stump out there, too. Every Yuletide we all get gifts of her homemade soap and shampoo—which is actually a real treat. My skin is much softer when I use her homespun products. I guess that's where I got my own crafting knack from.

I closed up the shop and biked home for a quick shower and change of clothes before I headed to Mom's. Then Selene and I piled into my car and made the short drive across town. Mom's house sits at the edge of a pond, with evergreen trees providing shade in the summer and a windbreak in the winter.

I parked in the driveway, noting my brother Evan's minivan was already in evidence. As I stepped out of my car, I became aware of a piercing shriek. Actually, two shrieks. A smile tugged the corners of my mouth as my nieces, Ruby and Emme, thundered around the corner of the house like a herd of tiny elephants.

"Hi, Auntie Cora!" they called in unison.

They were wielding fly swatters like swords, pretending to chase a dragon or some such. I felt a slight twinge of disgust; those fly swatters normally hung in my mother's kitchen, and let's just say they get put to a lot of use in the summer because Mom likes to cook with the back door open.

I waved at them on my way to the front porch, making a mental note not to allow the girls to "attack" me with the fly gut–spattered "swords," before stepping inside. The way things work around my Mom's house is that when you're expected, you don't bother knocking. It wasn't the home where I'd grown up. Mom had only bought this house about eight years ago, but even still, the place was bursting with some of my favorite memories. Home was wherever my family gathered.

I strode into the kitchen and found my mother flitting about, stirring this and flipping that and looking like a true maestro in her element. Her short gray hair belied her spryness. She paused to take a sip from a glass of wine on the counter and spotted me. "Hey there, Sunshine. How was the day?"

She paused long enough to give me a side hug, so as not to soil my garments with her used apron. "Oh, you know. Tail end of tourist season."

I pitched in a little to help with the cooking. Mom hardly needed my assistance, but she expressed gratitude to have it. As I poked around, I noticed a dark cake pan sitting off to the side and peeled back the layer of foil protecting it. "Are you making turtle brownies?"

"Hands off," she snapped playfully. "Don't let the twins know; they'll hound me relentlessly until those brownies come out of the oven if they find out."

I grinned. "And we know Grandma has a real big

problem with the N-O word when it comes to her little sunbeams."

Mom laughed. "Guilty as charged. I've waited my whole life to be a grandma and spoil my grandbabies rotten."

"And how do you feel about spoiling ancient protectors?" Selene asked, marching into the kitchen.

Mom smiled and gestured at the oven. "Don't worry, Selene. I've got your favorite already set to broiling."

"Excellent! See, Cora, you could learn a thing or two from your mother."

Mom and I exchanged a giggle behind the cat's back.

"Well, well, well, look who showed up. Fashionably late as ever," a male voice said.

I turned to find the grinning face of my brother, Evan. "Hey, Evs."

We hugged briefly and then he gave me a noogie, tousling my short hair every which way.

I smacked him on the arm and set about fixing it.

"Oh, you two. I swear, sometimes it's like you never advanced past the age of eight," Mom sighed.

"You two?" I repeated. "What did I do?"

We eventually all sat down to dinner, Cheyenne

and Evan wrangling their children and getting them to wash up first. I was glad to see the fly swatters had been dunked in the pond; at least that should wash off some of the fly guts.

While we dug into our salmon patties and mashed potatoes—Mom likes to use the gravy for both—I brought up the subject that had been bothering me. "Has anyone heard from Aunt Lavender recently?"

"Not since the end of June," Mom said, her face scrunching up in thought. "I remember trying to pin her down for our Fourth of July barbecue, and she was acting noncommittal, as usual."

"Why do you ask?" Evan's brows furrowed as he bit into a buttered biscuit.

"Selene went to her house today and said it's really overgrown. The city has been leaving notices on the porch. They're going to fine her if she doesn't clean it up soon."

"Hmm. I see." Mom dabbed at her mouth with a napkin and frowned. "You know how hard it is to get ahold of your aunt when she's off on one of her 'quests.' She won't even carry a cell phone, and if she did, how would she charge it?"

"Still, I can't help but feel a little worried."

Mom nodded. "I'll use the scrying mirror to see if I can't locate her after dinner."

Evan swigged some iced tea, then cleared his throat. "Tell you what, tomorrow after work, I'll stop by Lavender's place and see if I can't tidy it up."

"Are you sure you don't mind?" Mom asked.

"Of course not. It'll be nice to get some fresh air."

I smiled to myself, thinking it really meant he could spend an afternoon away from home, drinking his way through a couple of beers, without his wife or little girls interrupting.

"Maybe the girls could come, too," Cheyenne said, smiling at her husband. "You know they love to help, and I could really use a pedicure. I'll bet Trista could fit me in tomorrow."

Evan frowned, but Ruby and Emme were already bouncing around excited, so he couldn't burst their bubble.

"All right, but you owe me one," he told his wife before kissing her cheek.

Cheyenne beamed, victorious.

"Did you all see the paper this weekend?" Mom asked, changing the subject.

"Oh my goodness," Cheyenne said, shaking her head in sympathy. "That poor family."

"I can't believe they think his own brother did it," Evan added with a frown.

"Why don't you ask Cora?" Selene said smugly. "She knows all about it."

"Selene," I warned.

"The accused killer asked her for a date, and she said yes."

I rolled my eyes and tossed my dinnerware down in disgust.

"No way," Evan said, his eyes going wide. "And I thought your taste in men couldn't get any worse than that kid with the mullet in seventh grade—ow!"

Cheyenne poked her elbow into his ribs a bit gentler the second time, eyes glaring a warning.

"Atomic elbow by Mom!" Ruby shouted. Emme joined in her glee, clapping vigorously.

"Can we just talk about something else?" I sighed. "Please?"

"Well, dear, did you know Roger is back in town?" Mom poked into a pile of peas on her plate with exaggerated casualness.

"How do you know that?"

"So, you *did* know. He stopped by for a visit."

I smacked myself in the face and muttered. I couldn't win no matter what I did.

By the time I left Mom's house, my belly was

distended with a food baby, and I was laden with enough leftovers to feed an army. Why Mom always has to cook like she's feeding an entire football team I have no idea, but I never complained.

"I hope you're happy with yourself," I told Selene as we backed out of the driveway. "Thanks to your antics at dinner, these leftover salmon patties are all mine."

8

At the heart of it, Winterspell is a tourist town. Witches, wizards, shifters, and the occasional vampire come into town from all over to vacation in a place where they can let their supernatural freak flag fly. Its remote location, magical protection, and plethora of outdoor activities make it the perfect retreat from the non-magical world. On the weekends, the crystal-clear lake in the center of town is swarmed with kayakers, backpackers, campers, fishermen—you name it, people are doing it. The flood of visitors also means that during the summer months, I never get a weekend day off. Instead, I close my shop on Wednesdays to ensure at least one full day of rest and relaxation—though, more often than not, I just wind up working on new candle ideas at home in my spare bedroom turned workshop.

On the plus side, Wednesdays were usually less busy around town, even at the peak of tourist season, as a lot of people opted for a long weekend with Thursday, Friday or Monday, Tuesday as their bumper. So, it worked quite well. I didn't miss out on a lot of business and the lake was less congested. This was especially true now, as summer was fading, and schools were soon to be back in session.

I woke up that morning eager to put my troubles behind me in a literal and figurative sense, if only for a little while. Selene was still snoozing on her tufted pillow in the living room, so I quietly made my coffee and packed up what I'd need for the day, careful not to disturb her. I set out a bowl of her expensive kitty chow, and then went out to the garage to gather my equipment for a lengthy kayaking excursion.

I'm a seasoned vet when it comes to preparing for a kayaking trip. Extra paddle? Check. Paddle leash? Check. Compass and radio (both able to float)? Check and check. I even went the extra mile and took along my flare gun, in case I got lost while doing some hiking later in the afternoon. Though it was fairly unlikely I would become lost as I'd become quite accustomed to the trails around Winterspell.

I loaded up my kayak on top of my car and drove out to the big lake. The sun shone bright and hot, but I knew it would be cooler on the water. Mountain springs fed the lake via the small streams around Winterspell, tempering the summer's heat.

I parked the car and lugged my boat down to the water. I launched out onto the lake and paddled until I'd built up some momentum. I was one of a handful of people on the lake, and most of them were a good distance away. The surface remained calm and still, reflecting the beautiful mountains rearing up from the landscape with mirror-like perfection.

The lake, simply put, was my happy place. I couldn't think of anywhere I felt more free, more like myself, than being out on the water. Mom used to tease me that I'd been born under the wrong elemental sign. Elemental witches were generally granted their power based on when they were born. I was an air witch, having been born in the autumn. Air witches could have a range of powers, everything from telekinesis to weather magic to being a powerful tracker, or in my case, an illusionist. Other signs like water, earth, and fire all had their own expressions of power. And as with most attributes, magical or not, everyone had a varying degree. Some were blessed with an abundance of magical talent, while others could barely conjure so much as an orb of light while traversing a dark hallway.

Personally, I fell somewhere in the middle. I was never going to be a defensive magic expert, let alone engage in combat magic, but my illusion work was top notch. I'd even won several contests while in school and had an article in the *Winterspell Gazette* written about one of my magical fair projects. Still, I often thought my mother was right. There was something about the water that called to me, far more than wind ever did.

As the morning sun had only just risen, a fog bank clung to the center of the lake, where the water was coolest. I didn't mind paddling into its cool embrace. I knew the lake well, and I still had plenty of visibility to protect myself from collisions.

For a time I paddled through the gray, the sun a feeble white disk dimly visible through the fog bank. I felt almost as if I were flying through my own private cloud, and my mind drifted, unwinding like a ball of yarn tossed across the floor. Coils of tension and worry relaxed and sloughed away as I let myself fully relax into the morning and serene quiet.

Until I heard the sound of paddles in the water

that were not my own. An orange and black shape appeared, blurry from the mist. Another kayaker. I raised my hand for a friendly wave, and then I realized I knew the kayaker.

Roger. My ex-husband. I should have known he'd be out here. He likes kayaking almost as much as I do.

I hastily pulled a 180, nearly capsizing myself with the urgency of escape. I dropped the paddle and batted the water with my hands frantically until I went right side up again.

"Wow, déjà vu."

I grimaced as Roger pulled up abreast of me, a grin stretching his lips—which, I noted, were no longer being weighed down by that ridiculous mustache. "Reminds me of the first time we met. Only that time, you really did capsize," he added with a good-natured chuckle.

"That was hardly my fault," I replied, a touch of frost in my voice. "There was a freaking tsunami kicked up by an air witch parasailing that day, if you recall."

I was in no mood to wander down memory lane. I had come to the lake to kayak precisely to avoid thinking about my problems, not to have them paddling up to me. Still, since he was there, I decided to get something off my chest.

"Roger, what in the world made you think it was a good idea to just stop by my mother's house?"

"Lilac and I have always gotten along well. What's the harm in me stopping in to say hello?" His face scrunched up into an annoyed frown.

I couldn't think of a specific reason why it was a bad idea, which only annoyed me further. "I just wish you'd have left her out of it," I finally said.

Roger tilted his head to the side like a confused dog. "I'm confused. It's not like our relationship ended on a sour note, Cora. Or, at least, I didn't think it did." He paused, his gaze drifting for a moment. When he shifted his eyes back to mine, there was a sadness to them. "It seems like you're upset that I moved back to Winterspell."

Pain twisted in my chest. A pain I thought I'd banished months ago. It was almost worse somehow, seeing that Roger clearly didn't feel that same ache. For him, maybe it was just as simple as dissolving a business contract. Our divorce hurt me. Sure, I'd been the one to raise the topic of divorce, but in hindsight, I wondered if there was a piece of me that was hoping it would spur a revitalization of our relationship, rather than deliver the final kiss of death.

At the end of the day, Roger hadn't fought for our marriage, and while I suppose I didn't either, the way he left still stung. In any case, I knew for a fact I was not in a place where I wanted to discuss our marriage, and the way it ended.

"Never mind," I said, shaking my head. I changed the topic to kayaking, something we could both talk about for hours. Roger reluctantly took the hint and engaged in the lighter conversation as we paddled about the lake a couple of times before heading to shore.

When we reached the beach, Roger surprised me by offering a hand out of the boat. I accepted it, feeling strange that this was the first time I'd touched him in a year and a half. He returned his rental kayak to the lake house while I lugged mine back to the car. Roger trotted up to me as I was securing it to my roof.

"Hey, Cora," he said, not the least out of breath from his jog. Roger always had kept himself in great shape. "I wanted to ask you something."

"Yes?" I turned to him and waited.

"You want to grab some lunch? My treat. We still

haven't had a chance to catch up since I returned to town."

I tensed up. I really didn't want to deal with Roger or all of the emotions his appearance had churned up inside of me. "I'm sorry, I've got a lot of work to catch up on at the shop."

"Oh. Okay." Roger couldn't fully hide his disappointment. "Some other time, then."

I retreated by way of climbing inside the car and starting the engine. I wasn't fibbing when I told Roger I had a lot of work to catch up on. I could spread out my workstation and really get down to business when the shop was closed.

I stopped by Whimzee's Deli for lunch, winding up with a Reuben sandwich on marble rye with a Caesar salad on the side. Whimzee's sandwiches are huge, but I could have half of it for dinner.

I headed into the shop through the back way and settled down for a busy day of crafting magical artifacts. Selene showed up sometime around two o'clock, slipping in through the back door, which I left cracked in hopes of catching a breeze. She leaped up on the counter and licked a bit of dressing from my sandwich wrapper without so much as a *hello*.

I scratched behind her ears while I waited for my wax to heat up. Most of the ingredients for candle magic are surprisingly mundane. There's no pixie dust or dragon's teeth needed—though to be honest I could make much more potent candles if I had such things, but I digress.

I harvested most of my raw ingredients from the woods surrounding Winterspell. I'd found that a fishing tackle box was the perfect receptacle for all of my supplies. I reached into a bin filled with wick washers between bites of my lunch, rummaging about until I found one the appropriate size.

A knock came at the shop's front door. I froze mid-chew.

"Who could that be?" I swallowed the bite of food and stood up from my stool, wiping my fingers on a paper napkin as I headed for the front of the shop. "Delivery or something?"

I stepped through the archway and my jaw nearly hit the floor when I saw Clint standing there.

Tossing the sullied napkin aside, I hurried to unlock and open the front door. "Clint?"

He looked a bit less haggard than he had the other day, and I noticed he had my laptop in his hand. "Hey," he said softly, a sheepish smile on his face. "Sorry to run off the other day. I sort of panicked." He passed the laptop to me. "Here's this back. I appreciate it so much."

I glared at him. "You know, I was planning on lending it to you. You didn't need to run off with it like that."

Clint cocked an eyebrow. "Wait, what? Did you think I stole it?"

He dropped his gaze to the floor by my feet, where Selene had sauntered up. "I told your cat that I would be back to drop it off. She was supposed to tell you."

Selene's tail twitched in annoyance. "Do I look like a receptionist? Or a messenger service? Seriously."

"Sometimes I wonder what you actually are good for," I muttered. I turned back to Clint. "I heard something the other day that might help your case."

His brows climbed halfway up his forehead. I decided he was just a tad handsomer than Roger, but Roger had a better physique. Then I immediately felt shallow and superficial for even thinking such a thing. Still, while the word "dreamy" gets tossed around a lot, Clint certainly fit the bill.

"You did? What was it?"

I shook the cobwebs out of my head. I hadn't realized he'd spoken for a moment. "Oh, well, when I was at book club, I heard your brother Seth was having an affair with a much younger woman. Apparently, a barmaid at a local tavern."

Clint heaved a sigh. "I hate to say this, but it wouldn't surprise me. My brother has cheated on just about every woman he's had a relationship with. I honestly thought maybe he'd changed, though. Melissa seems different than some of his past exes." He paused and shook his head. "Sorry, I don't mean to dump more of my family's drama onto you. I appreciate you telling me this."

"It might be relevant to the case," I said. "That's the only reason I bring it up. Maybe this lover got jealous. Maybe he was promising to leave his wife, and then she got pregnant, so he backed out of his promise."

"I'm not sure I'm in a position to ask them about the investigation, but I'll bring it up to my lawyer. He's the only one speaking to them on my behalf presently."

I nodded. "That's probably a good idea. Anyway, I just thought maybe it was something you should know."

Clint dropped his gaze to the pavement for a moment before looking me in the eye again. The vulnerable light in his eyes made my heart skip a beat. "Honestly, Cora, I feel like you're the only one I can trust in this town."

He gave a derisive chuckle, the sardonic edge directed squarely at himself. "Heck, I think you're the only one I can trust, period."

"Why is that?" I asked.

"Well, it's just … I'm a workaholic. Everybody knows it. I've been quite successful, but it's left me largely cut off from my life back home, my … family. I don't have a lot of close friends, you know? And the friends that I do have, well … they're human. I can't exactly share my current predicament with them. They think I'm an only child, a silver-spoon trust fund kid from upstate New York. They have no idea about Winterspell, or … well, any of this."

"What about your mother?"

Clint heaved a heavy sigh. "She's refusing my calls. I tried to go to her house, and the maid told me she didn't want to see me."

"I'm sorry. That must be hard for you to bear." Once again, I was struck by the fact that he didn't seem like a killer.

"Yeah." He looked off down the street and sighed.

"How did things go with your client?"

He let out a short, derisive bark of laughter. "The

deal fell through. I guess this is what rock bottom feels like."

"Hey, tall, dark, and gloomy."

We looked down at Selene. "Have you forgotten that I have the recipe for a spell that will help you out of your current situation?"

I put my hands on my hips. "You know, Selene, it's not nice to tease someone when they're down."

"Who's teasing?" The cat's ears went back. "I'm surprised at you. While I am a tad bit difficult at times—"

"A *tad* bit?" I sputtered. "At times?"

"—but I never lie about magic. Trust me. I've got just the thing this situation requires."

I sighed. "All right, hit us with it. What do you know that can help?"

"Necromancy," Selene said, and a chill wind blew right then, though I think it might have been from me. The very word seemed to drop my body temperature a few degrees.

"Selene—"

"I have the recipe for a spell to cross the universe divide and contact Seth's spirit. Then you can get the skinny straight from the horse's mouth. The dead horse's mouth."

Clint turned to me. "Would that work? I mean, is that actually a thing?"

I hesitated to answer. "I've heard of such spells before, though I don't know any."

"Good thing you don't need to know the spells," Selene replied. "All you'll have to do is repeat after me."

"Gee, what could go wrong?" I muttered.

"Cora? Could this actually work?" Clint asked, a layer of desperation creeping into his voice.

I cringed as I looked down at Selene. "P—probably, but—"

"Probably?" Selene huffed indignantly.

I didn't want to get involved in a murder investigation. And I *really* did not want to get involved with necromancy magic. But ... I felt sorry for Clint. At the moment, he had no one in all the world, not even his own family.

"Oh, come on, Cora. Where is your sense of adventure?" Selene scoffed. "What's the use of magic if it can't help out a friend? I'm assuming that's a fair definition for the two of you, otherwise you would have called the coppers by now to come round him up."

"Well, I—" Squeezing my eyes tight, I drew in a deep

breath and pushed aside my swirling thoughts. When I opened them again, Clint's dark eyes were staring back at me, intense and pleading. With a heavy exhale, I nodded. "Okay. Fine. If Selene is willing to share her knowledge, then I'm willing to assist you in this."

"You will?" Gratitude writ itself large across his handsome face. "I really appreciate that, thank you."

"Excellent," Selene purred. "Now, as to the matter of payment."

I frowned. "Oh boy, here it comes."

"I'm quite tired of using a plastic litter pan," Selene began, "especially the cheap, shallow one Cora purchased when I moved in. It's come to my attention that there is something called a Cyber-Litter 5000 on the market—"

"Selene, that thing costs nearly a thousand dollars!"

Selene twitched her tail. "As I said, magic comes with a price tag. In this case, nine-hundred and forty-eight dollars, or if you prefer, six easy payments of—"

"We can do the math," I said, cutting off her sales pitch. "But, get real. There's no way—"

"I'll buy it," Clint interrupted.

My eyes widened.

Selene grinned. "I knew I liked you."

"You're sure?" I asked Clint.

He nodded. "I said I would do whatever it takes."

"Now," Selene continued, rising to her feet, "we're going to need some rather hard-to-acquire spell components to pull this off."

I cursed silently. "There's always something. All right, what do we do about that? Please tell me it doesn't involve grave digging."

Selene's whiskers twitched. "Ugh! What do you take me for, Cora?"

I didn't answer her.

The cat stood and began marching toward the back room of my shop. "Lavender has most everything we'll need at her house. We can raid her stores."

I sighed. "I suppose we should check on the place anyway …"

"See? It all worked out."

We made plans to meet the next night. I hoped, most sincerely, that I was not making a mistake.

*M*y aunt Lavender had always been something of a flighty presence in my life. As a child, she'd taken me under her wing and taught me things I didn't learn in school. We'd go for walks in the woods, and she carefully explained which mushrooms cured ills, which were deadly poisons, and which ones were fun for parties —though Mom quickly stepped in to correct that last part of the lessons. Even now, I can go walking in the woods and my brain will catalogue every leaf, every root, and every nut along the way, judging their potency for curative and spell effects.

Lavender was a great teacher, when she was around. The problem was, she had trouble focusing on any one thing for too long a time. Sometimes I'd ride my bike to her house for a lesson, and find that she had gone, having jaunted off on some new misadventure for King Arthur's codpiece or the lost spindle to the Wheel of Time. Luckily, her neighbor at the time, Mrs. Lewis, had a good radar for these situations and invited me over for cookies and lemonade before sending me back home again.

Over time, I grew used to Lavender's flighty ways, but I also grew resentful of being forgotten over and over again. She missed all of my important milestone occasions: magic fairs, swim meets, my graduation, and perhaps most painful of all, even my wedding to Roger. Mom got onto her case about it a few times, quite a few times in fact, but despite earnest-sounding promises to change, sooner or later Lavender had to be Lavender and would vanish once more.

My last memory of her was from nearly four years ago. Despite living in the same town, I'd stopped bothering to visit or keep up with her. The last time I'd visited her, we'd been mid conversation, when she went outside and seemingly vanished. She'd stopped coming to family dinners at my mom's house, mostly because she didn't keep a calendar and would always forget.

I missed my aunt, but it was perhaps more that I

missed who she could have been, if she'd simply stayed in one place and tried to be better. To be present, instead of living with one foot constantly out the door, her mind off on her next adventure before her physical body could follow.

So, it was with mixed emotions that I pulled up outside of Lavender's bungalow-style home the following evening with Clint and Selene. I stared at the house, painted black but faded to gray in the light of the sun. The weeds and high grass choked the front yard, just as Selene had reported. As I watched, a cloud of gnats played in a beam of sun penetrating the virtual jungle's thick blades.

"You weren't kidding," I said, nose wrinkling in disgust. I looked about the sleepy little neighborhood and saw nothing but neatly trimmed lawns and manicured bushes. I figured it was probably the worst possible neighborhood for someone like Lavender to live in, but she had been there for decades and wouldn't consider moving. "Looks like Evan got distracted and forgot about coming over to mow," I commented as we picked our way through the overgrown yard toward the front porch.

Clint ducked under an angry wasp's dive bomb attack and slapped a mosquito trying to munch on his neck. "No wonder the neighbors are complaining. It's like a wild safari out here."

I chuckled and produced a slight breeze, just strong enough to blow back the smaller, peskier bugs. We stepped up onto her spacious front porch, my conjured breeze causing it to rock gently in the wind.

I tried the door, and found it locked. "Of course. I should have expected this."

"You should have expected what?" Clint frowned as I stood back from the door.

"Aunt Lavender never leaves her home unprotected. She always leaves it Witch Locked."

"Witch locked? What does that mean? Remember, I don't get out here to Winterspell much. Where I'm from, we use triple deadbolts."

"It means we need to figure out how to convince the house to let us in." I scratched my chin and noticed my aunt had done some painting recently. Beside the door, the house's siding had been scrawled with magical glyphs and runes in fresh black paint that stood out from the faded paint. "This looks new."

"It is," Selene said, padding up to sniff at the sigils. "Want to know how to get the door open?"

"Yes, please."

"Take a good look at the sigils."

I squinted, and then chuckled. "It's a riddle, written in High Faerie. 'As I was going to St. Ives, in fact,'" I read.

"St. Ives?" Clint repeated.

"Seriously?" Selene sighed, and then recited the rest of the clue:

As I was going to St. Ives,
I met a man with seven wives,
Each wife had seven sacks,
Each sack had seven cats,
Each cat had seven kits:
Kits, cats, sacks, and wives,
How many were there going to St. Ives?

"Oh man," Clint said, his face contorting in a grimace of concentration. "That's a tough one. If I had my phone, I'd bust out the calculator, but I think I can do this in my head."

I covered my mouth with my hand to hide my smile and stifle a laugh as Clint started counting off on his fingers. Selene looked pleased as punch. This was exactly the outcome she'd wanted.

"Um, so it's seven times, what, five?" he clapped his hands. "The answer is thirty-five."

"I'm afraid not," I said and prepared to knock on the door. "Think about it. The answer is one."

"One? That doesn't make any sense."

Selene's eyes glittered with amusement. "Yes, it does. Shall I recite it for you again?"

"Not now, Selene," I said, taking a deep breath. "All I have to do is knock the appropriate number of times, and the house will let us in. In this case, that's one."

"Are you sure?" Clint asked.

"Positive … mostly."

"Wait," he said as I lifted my fist. "What happens if you knock the wrong number of times?"

Selene's blue eyes gleamed as she looked up at him. "Well, Lavender had a penchant for transporting would-be thieves into the caldera of an active volcano, but she's hopefully mellowed with age."

"What?!"

Laughing, I rapped one time on the door and waited. The runes on the wall glowed, startling Clint once again, and the door swung open.

"Easy peasy." I pushed the door fully open or tried to. It hit something and wouldn't budge any further. "I should warn you, my aunt Lavender is something of a hoarder."

I squeezed inside the bungalow, finding that the barrier preventing the door's movement was a stack of *National Geographic* magazines piled to the ten-foot ceiling. There were more stacks of magazines immediately flanking the front door, forming a kind of hallway.

"Come on. Don't worry, it's cluttered and a bit claustrophobic but Aunt Lavender would never let it get gross. There's no roaches or rats to worry about, but you might run into the occasional spider."

"Are you afraid of spiders, Clint?" Selene asked with a wicked smile.

"Who isn't?" He stepped over a stack of leather-bound spell books that had collapsed in the makeshift hallway. "I can't even tell which part of the house we're in."

"This is the living room. Passage splits up ahead, at the spools of thread. To the left is the bathroom and kitchen, to the right the bedroom."

I sidled through the magazines and books until I came upon a veritable fortress made of Velveeta cheese blocks. That stuff has the same half-life as uranium, and Lavender was always stockpiling it for … whatever reason.

"She certainly likes cheese."

"Yeah, you should have seen Cora when she spent a month living on nothing but mac and cheese. Constipation like the world has never known—"

"TMI, Selene!" I turned to Clint and sighed. "I'm sorry it's such a mess."

"No, it's fine. Like you said, it's not dirty, just, uh, a little dusty—"

Clint shrieked and jumped about a foot. Selene laughed, flicking her tail as she stood atop the cheese tower. "Ha! You thought the brush of my tail on the back of your neck was a creepy little spider, didn't you, Clint?"

"Selene, can you try not to give him a heart attack? The goddess knows there isn't room in here for a team of paramedics to work." I shook my head in dismay. "What do we need for the spell?"

"We need the silver tea service from the kitchen, Lavender's potion kit, some silver-infused chalk, and a vial of cobra venom. She keeps it in the fridge. You can't miss it."

I grimaced.

"Oh, and the catnip-infused cat treats. Definitely need those," Selene added before jumping to the top of a buried piano in the corner.

"Right, of course." I rolled my eyes. "Listen, Clint, I'll gather everything up. Try not to get lost. You may never return."

Clint laughed, but it trailed off when I didn't join him. He turned to Selene. "She's joking, right?"

"Well, there might be the corpse of a vacuum cleaner salesman in here somewhere, but I'll never tell."

I shook my head in helplessness at Selene's continued ribbing of Clint. I found the tea service, venom, and potion kit easily enough, but the chalk proved difficult to locate. I wound up digging through boxes filled with every assortment of junk one could imagine, and quite a few that would be impossible to.

In Lavender's bedroom, I discovered one clear spot besides her bed, an area on the far wall. My mouth fell open when I saw, atop an overstuffed bookcase, a space cleared out for a photo of myself and Evan when we were in our early twenties. The picture had been taken at a family reunion Mom hosted out at the campgrounds. Lavender had only remembered to show up on the last day, when most of our extended family had already departed to get back home. I could clearly recall the crestfallen look on her face when she realized her mistake and felt a stab of guilt. I really should visit her more often. Sure she was unreliable, but her quirky tendencies were part of what made Lavender … well, Lavender.

Besides, she obviously cared more than she let on. With a final glance at the photograph, I sighed and turned to find Selene padding into the room. The cat looked up at me, and for a moment, I was more than a little worried about what Lavender might say when she returned from her latest quest and found that I had taken custody of her familiar. Would she see it as a betrayal and cut me out of her life entirely? Then a second thought hit, and with a sick feeling in my stomach, I wondered how that would really make a difference at this point.

"I can't find the chalk," I told Selene as I dropped to my knees beside the bed. I looked underneath it.

"Yikes. I'd be careful under there," Selene said. "Spiders might not be the only things that have moved in since Lavender left."

"Wait a minute." I reached out and grabbed a thin, leather case. Frowning, I pulled it out from under the bed and held it up for Selene to see. "Look. It's Lavender's specimen case."

"So?"

"So? She never leaves on an excursion without it. At least, she never has before, that I know of."

Selene's tail began to twitch. "You know, now that you mention it, she didn't take her first aid kit either. It was still on the bathroom shelf. That's always one of the first things she packs."

"She barely goes to the grocery store without that

thing," I muttered, shaking my head. "I wonder what she was thinking."

"Don't know."

I rummaged about until I found the silver-infused chalk in the overstuffed drawer of her bedside table. I suppose I could have purchased some more at the magical supply shop, but like her soap and shampoo, Lavender made her own chalk. If she thought it needed custom ingredients, who was I to argue with her?

At last, I'd gathered all I would need for the spell, though I was dubious as to what purpose the catnip-infused treats could possibly serve. I collected Clint, who had become embroiled in one of Lavender's spell-casting books. He glanced up and eyed the collection of items in my arms. "Are we all set?"

"Yes. I think maybe it would be best if we did the spell at my place, though."

Clint laughed. "There's not much room here, no."

I loaded up the car, and then cursed myself silently because I remembered I hadn't cleaned my house in about a week. Like Aunt Lavender, I didn't leave dirty dishes or food lying about, but I was certain there would be a few dust bunnies.

Then again, with what Clint endured in Aunt

Lavender's house, I supposed a couple of dust bunnies wouldn't be the thing to scare him off.

My anxiety spiked as we pulled into the driveway. "Um, listen, I'm not the world's best housekeeper, and I've been really busy—"

"Don't sweat it. How can I complain after you've helped me so much? Besides, you should have seen my first bachelor pad."

"No, something tells me it's a very good thing I never beheld it," I said with a laugh. "I still remember the state of my brother's bachelor pad back in the day and let me just say … ewwww. My sister-in-law should be sainted or knighted or something for taming that hot mess."

Clint smiled as we took the steps up to the front door. "I didn't know you had a brother."

I paused, my fingers freezing on my keyring, as I realized the implication. "Oh, I'm sorry, I shouldn't be talking about my brother when yours is—"

Clint stopped me with a gentle hand on my arm. "No, no, Cora, please. I don't mind. Are you the elder sibling?"

With a nervous smile, I shook my head. "Younger. Evan is four years older than me. I'll be thirty-five on my next birthday, and he just turned thirty-nine. He's married and has two girls, twins. My nieces, Ruby and Emme. They're five."

"Sounds nice," Clint said with a warm grin, despite the sad look in his eyes.

I unlocked the deadbolt and swung it open. From my place at the front door, I spied a stray bra on the sofa, likely discarded at the end of a very long work-day, and quickly blew a puff of wind to send it flying down the hallway, out of sight, before stepping inside and allowing Clint entrance.

"Hey," I asked, "are you hungry? I don't have a lot of groceries in the house, but I'm sure I could whip up something for us."

"I could eat, but I don't want you to go to any trouble."

"Not at all." I busied myself in the kitchen while he sat down at the table. "How does some leftover tuna salad sound?"

"Sounds great."

I busied myself with the meal preparation while we chatted. With brioche toasting in the oven, I peppered him with questions regarding his life outside of Winterspell, in an attempt to get his mind off the investigation and his brother's death.

Clint indulged me, discussing his consulting business back in Chicago. It sounded like he wasn't kidding when he'd described himself as a workaholic. When I asked about hobbies or activities outside of the office, he hesitated for a long moment before half-heartedly saying he enjoyed the occasional round of golf. Something about the way he said it made me think he only played when necessary to hammer out a business deal or treat special clients.

When the brioche was ready, I took it out of the oven, brushed it down with some grass-fed butter from a local farm, and then divvied it up between us. I set the bowl of tuna salad on the table and we took turns spreading it on our toast. The first bite was pure heaven.

"This is pretty good," Clint said. "Delicious, in fact."

"Thanks. I'm not a maestro in the kitchen by any stretch, but I learned to get by when I was younger. My mom is an excellent cook, but growing up, she was a single mom and didn't have a lot of time to prepare big meals every night. Now that she's retired though—look out! She treats our biweekly family dinners like one of those competitive cooking shows on the Food Network, and makes enough to feed the entire neighborhood."

Clint smiled. "It sounds like she's doing what she loves."

"Definitely." I nodded and took another bite.

"My mother wouldn't know a caper from a split pea, I'm afraid. Growing up there was a personal chef to manage the kitchen, a pair of full-time housekeepers, a gardener, and a nanny." Clint paused for a dry, humorless laugh. "As an adult, I wonder just what it was she actually *did* all day while Seth and I were off at boarding school or under the care of Paula, our nanny. Probably off at the spa, or some formal ladies' luncheon."

He shook his head, seemingly lost in thought.

We were saved from an awkward silence by a blue-eyed cat leaping onto the counter. She looked at us pointedly and said, "Are you ready to talk to this dead guy yet, or what?"

10

"*O*f course we're ready." Clint rubbed his hands together eagerly. "All right. How do we do this? This magic thing, I mean."

Selene's tail twitched back and forth. "Well, *you* are going to shut up and do whatever we tell you to, that's what you're going to do. Leave the spell casting to the experts."

"Selene, don't be rude. Besides, they say that the most confident people are also the most modest."

"Sounds like something a hairless ape came up with. If you've got it, flaunt it. That's what I always say."

"Before or after you cough up a hairball?" I muttered.

"First things first," Selene said, ignoring my jab.

"We're going to have to brew some tea, with a very special ingredient."

"For heaven's sake, Selene. You said we had everything we needed from Aunt Lavender's place." I glared at the gray cat sitting on my kitchen island. "If we have to go back—"

"No one has to go back, don't get your panties in a bunch." Selene's ears flattened against her furry head. "No, the special ingredient is close at hand, I assure you. In fact, it's standing right there in a pair of overpriced Italian loafers."

She turned her blue-eyed gaze pointedly on Clint. He blinked in confusion, then looked at me. "Me? What possible—I don't even know how to do much magic."

"Relax, twinkle toes," Selene said. "You don't have to do anything. You do, however, need to provide us with our missing ingredient."

"What's that?"

"Your blood, of course." Selene's eyes narrowed on Clint. "We need some way to connect you to your sibling. Otherwise, the spell will be like a streetlight with regard to bugs. We'd attract every type of random ghost you could name without ever finding the one we want."

"My blood ..." Clint swallowed hard. "How much?"

"Oh, a couple of gallons at least."

Clint's eyes bugged out of his head. "A couple of gallons? Are you out of your mind?"

"Relax, we'll leave you some," Selene said.

I turned a suspicious eye on the familiar. "Selene, come on, get serious."

"What makes you think I'm not being serious?" Selene was the portrait of innocence. And when Selene was the portrait of innocence, I got very, very suspicious.

"Well, for one thing, you couldn't even get a half gallon of anything in that silver teapot ..."

"Ha! Look who put on her thinking cap today. Well done, Cora. Now, if we could only get this one firing on all cylinders," she said, casting a look at Clint. Sighing, as though he were a lost cause, she continued, "We only need a drop or two."

She leaped to the kitchen counter—which was usually a big no-no—and began peering around the contents of Lavender's potion kit. "Now, did you see where that spoon got off to?"

"This one?" I picked up an old-fashioned hammered copper spoon. Rustic and utilitarian, it exuded a vintage aura. I felt the stirrings of magic and realized it had been used for rituals in the past.

"Yeah, that's the one. We have to use that to harvest the blood."

"You … want me to cut him with a spoon?" I looked at the device incredulously.

Selene spoke a word and the metal seemed to melt, until the end of the spoon tapered into a very fine point, almost like a needle.

"Oh!" I grimaced. Something about a magical spoon that could turn into shiv at a moment's notice was more than a little unsettling. "Um, okay. Can you roll up your sleeve?"

Clint visibly swallowed but didn't argue. With a leery look, he undid his cufflink and rolled up his sleeve. Once his arm was bare, I lowered the needle toward his skin—

"Are you an idiot?" Selene walked over and circled a bottle of rubbing alcohol. "Sterilize the area first. Geez! I pulled this spoon out of Lavender's house and carried it here in my mouth for Merlin's sake."

"Oh. Good idea."

"Yeah, of course it was. By the way, Clint, when was the last time you had a tetanus shot?"

"I don't recall. Do I need one?" His brows furrowed in confusion.

Selene flicked the tip of her tail. "Eh, I'm sure it will be fine."

I used a folded-up paper towel to administer the rubbing alcohol. Clint tensed up as the needle neared his skin. I could tell he was trying to tough it out for appearances' sake. When the needle almost touched his skin, he turned his eyes away at the very last moment.

The needle punctured his skin and I removed it quickly. A little blood trickled out, and I glanced around for something to collect it in, kicking myself for not being more prepared. Suddenly, the spoon in my hand morphed again, and a perfectly round bead of blood sat in the now ladle-shaped end. "What the—"

"Get the man a tissue," Selene scolded. "We don't need him dripping all over the floor. I eat down there!"

"Here," I said, offering Clint a clean paper towel to staunch the bleeding.

Selene relaxed and guided me through the next step. "All right, now hang onto that, we won't add it until after the tea leaves steep for at least two minutes."

"Wait, you mean I have to hold this thing the whole time while the kettle heats up? Why didn't we get the blood last?"

"Hmm. Good point, that probably would have been smarter. This reminds me of the time Benjamin Franklin forgot to pack his glass harmonica. Musta been right before the Battle of Bennington—which wasn't even fought in Bennington, by the way—"

"Selene, let's not get off topic."

The kettle soon whistled, and I sprinkled the white tea leaves in the cup of steaming water and had Clint set a timer on the microwave. I added the venom and a few other ingredients in the order Selene prescribed. Once the concoction steeped the allotted time, I stirred in the single drop of blood and then set the spoon aside. "All right, what now?"

"Now we're going to summon Clint's dead brother. Think of the cup of tea like a two-way ticket: the drop of blood calls him to us, and the cobra venom sends him back to the Shadow Realm."

"Are you sure we'll get Seth?" Clint asked.

"Of course," Selene snapped. "I mean, how many dead relatives do you really think are kicking around near our plane of existence, anyway?" Selene turned to me. "You get to do this next part of the spell.

136

Remember the incantation I taught you on the way home?"

I nodded, then spoke the words of the spell in the old Witch Tongue. Clint frowned in confusion. I took it he didn't understand the words I said. If he had, he would have heard a long and flowery invitation to Seth Bridges to join us for tea. Sometimes magic isn't as complicated as it seems.

We waited a moment. Nothing visible happened, but I could feel a chill wind, a sure sign we were in contact with the Shadow Realm, the domain of ghosts and spirits stuck between this world and the Stardust Realm. Gradually, a grayish mist formed opposite the cup of tea. Clint sat forward eagerly, eyes wide with excitement.

"It's working!"

"Of course it's working," Selene sniffed. "You sound like you're surprised for some reason."

The mist coalesced, and grew denser, until it took on a definite man-like shape. I watched as features began to form: a nose, eyes, ears, bald spot, heavy jowls …

"Wait a minute," I said. "That's not Seth. Or at least, it's not the same man as in the photo I saw in the paper."

"That isn't Seth," Clint said, eyes narrowing to

slits as he leaned forward to scrutinize the apparition.

"Then who is it?"

"I think it's my grandfather. I haven't seen him since I was a kid, though."

A translucent, vaguely grayish figure now stood in my kitchen. He wore a suit that was a good size too small, the buttons on the jacket stretched to their limit, and a cigar jutted out of his mouth.

"What's this all about?" the ghost asked, removing the stogie from his lips for a moment.

"Uh, I'm sorry, I didn't actually want anything with *you*," I said, glancing at Selene, hoping she would step in.

"Then why did you ask me to tea? Not that I even like tea, but I thought I should come and see what you wanted." The ghost turned to Clint and his eyes went wide. "Little Clinton? Is that you? How long have I been gone?"

Clint winced. "Granddad, you know I hate being called Clinton."

"What's wrong with Clinton? It's a fine name, goes back a long time in our family." He looked about the kitchen. "I don't recognize half of the gadgets in this place. What is it with you youngsters and your toys? What's that one—some kind of blender? Your grandmother always was nagging me for one of those."

"Uh, that's a coffee grinder?" I suggested, assuming that was what he meant.

The ghost scoffed. "Now why would anyone want to buy a coffee grinder when they can just get themselves a canister of Sanka at the grocery store?"

Clint cleared his throat. "Um, no offense, Grand-dad, but have you seen Seth?"

The specter glanced over his shoulder. "He's around here somewhere. He won't stop bellyaching about his bad luck. I keep telling him to let it go, it's the only way to move on to the next level, but he won't listen. If he doesn't change his tune, he'll wind up like me. Of course, after all this time, I'm not sure I want to leave. The Shadow Realm isn't all bad, you know."

"That's good to hear," Clint said. "You have friends there?"

"Oh, sure. There's never a shortage of card sharks. We play a lot of poker."

Clint smiled, the answer seeming to genuinely please him. "You always were a tough one to beat."

The ghost beamed with pride and took another puff from the cigar. "Thank you, my boy."

"Listen, I don't know how much time we have.

So, could you go and get Seth for me? Can you bring him here?"

Gramps snorted. "I see how it is. You haven't even been to my grave since you were twelve, and now you want me to do you a favor?"

"Uh …" Clint cleared his throat, looking quite sheepish. "Yes?"

"I'm only teasing, Clinton, my boy. I'm glad you have a life. Live it to the fullest. I'll be here to catch up when you're done. Maybe we can play a hand of Texas Hold 'Em before you shuffle on to the Stardust Realm."

"I'd like that, Granddad." Clint smiled.

"All right, let me go find your whiny brother."

The ghost vanished in a puff of smoke. I turned to Selene and quirked an eyebrow.

"What?" she asked.

"This isn't going nearly as smoothly as you promised."

"It'll work, trust me."

I pursed my lips. "If it doesn't you can forget about your CyberLitter 5000."

"Hey! I'm a cat of my word. Don't you go reneging when this works like a charm."

"Shh!" I pointed at the new spot of mist that had

begun to form across my counter. "Someone's coming. Let's hope it's Seth."

Clint sat up straight, his eyes serious and hard. Gradually features began to appear, just like last time. Only this time around, it really was Seth who appeared.

"Seth …" Clint swallowed hard. "I'm so sorry for what happened to you."

"You're sorry?" Seth's ghostly eyes narrowed. "For what? Were you the one who put me here?"

"No!" Clint shook his head vehemently. Then his eyes widened. "Wait, you don't know who killed you? How is that possible?"

Seth's translucent hand moved up to cover his ectoplasmic face. Though ghosts don't have a corporeal form to speak of, they often act as if they do. Selene had explained it in the car. She said that there is something of a phantom period, where ghosts forget they aren't human, and will continue to walk around furniture and living people, even though they could pass right through them. It seemed Seth was still in that phase, which was understandable. He hadn't even been dead a week.

The ghost shook his head. "I just don't remember. I'm sorry. One minute I was there, and then …"

I cleared my throat. "Seth?"

He raised his—dare I say haunted?—gaze to meet my own.

"Yes?"

"Maybe it would help if you started at the beginning."

"What do you mean?"

"Well, what happened when you came home for the, uh, last time?"

Seth's ghostly eyes grew distant. When he spoke, his voice had dropped an octave. "I … got home from the office and headed right for the wine rack. I really needed a drink. I made myself a glass of chardonnay and headed into my study to relax."

"Why did you need to relax?"

His translucent brow furrowed in thought. "I'd had an argument with my business partner. A really nasty one."

Clint and I gave each other a look. Money is the root of all evil, or so they say. It wouldn't be the first time someone had murdered their business partner.

"What else do you remember?" I prompted Seth.

"Well … not much else. I put a Marty Robbins vinyl on the turntable. 'Big Iron' was playing, and I had drunk about half the glass of chardonnay. I don't remember what time it was, but I know it was early evening. I think …"

He rubbed the back of his head, the exact spot where the candlestick had done him in, I assumed.

"I'm sorry. I just don't remember."

"Seth," I asked, "was there anyone else in the house with you at the time?"

"No," Seth replied, shaking his head. "Melissa was out running errands."

"Man," Clint said. "I was really hoping you knew what happened to you, Seth. The cops think I did it."

Seth's face contorted in a sneer. "I don't know, Clint. That seems like a pretty good line of reasoning to me, especially after Mom cut you out of the will."

"She didn't cut me out of the will! Well, not completely, anyway. But it doesn't matter in any case; I've got plenty of money on my own."

"So you say, but you were always a greedy little kid when we were growing up." Seth sneered. "You were never satisfied with anything, you always had to have a little bit more."

Clint looked at me as if asking me to explain his brother's behavior. "I can't believe what I'm hearing. Are you kidding me? *I'm* greedy? Me? I don't think so! Let's swing that judgmental pendulum back your way, Seth. You're the one who can't get enough, judging by the way you've been running around town with your twenty-something side piece."

"How dare you!" Seth bellowed. "You know, I would have thought my own brother would be a little more sympathetic to my plight. I died too young! I'll never accomplish any of the things I wanted to do in my life."

"You married a good woman," Clint offered.

"Oh please," Seth sneered. "Anybody can get married. I wanted to climb Mt. Everest, and ski the Swiss Alps, and, and publish a novel before I died. Now I won't get to do any of that."

"Seth, you've never uttered one word about wanting to climb a mountain anywhere." Clint glared at his dead brother. "Not only that, but you hate skiing. You always get a cold and wind up sulking in the lodge getting falling-down drunk."

"How dare you! I'm quite literally the victim here. The murder victim! It's not fair. I was supposed to do so much more, to *be* so much more. Now, it's all over." Seth's face screwed up in disgust. "Do you know what the afterlife is like? Boring! Gray! Everything you look at is gray. I can't stand it."

"So move on to the next plane of existence," Selene suggested.

"I don't want to! I want to find a way back. It's

not fair. Clint's not married, *he* doesn't have a child on the way. He's the one who should have been killed."

"Are you kidding me?" I gasped. "That's an awful thing to say to your brother."

"Well, he's kind of an awful brother. Haven't even seen him in years. It's not fair. It's not fair! I wasn't ready! I had so much left to do! I—"

With a muttered word, Selene reached out and knocked the cup of tea off the counter. It fell to the floor and shattered. Instantly, Seth disappeared back into the Shadow Realm.

I looked at the cat for an explanation. She rolled one shoulder. "I was bored with his whining."

11

*S*elene crouched on the back of the sofa, peering over my shoulder at the laptop's glowing screen. The sun had just kissed the horizon, bringing night to Winterspell, but I had yet to turn on the lights in the living room. The glow of the screen provided the sole illumination other than the fading sunlight, bathing the room in shadow.

"That's it!" Selene said, tail darting back and forth. "That's the one. CyberLitter 5000."

I moved the cursor over the picture of a roughly bowl-shaped cylinder filled with a layer of litter. A product video played, featuring an Arnold Schwarzenegger lookalike in black leather wielding a shotgun.

"I am on a mission from the future," he said with

an obviously fake accent, dramatic music playing in the background. "A mission to terminate … ghastly litter odors."

He cocked the shotgun and fired it at a conventional litter box, which quite frankly looked like it hadn't been attended to in six months. The litter box exploded and the CyberLitter 5000 materialized in its place with a crackle of lighting.

The shot switched to "Arnold" holding up a furry cat. "Doesn't your fur baby deserve a fresh batch of litter every time they need to go potty? Don't delay. Terminate litter odor today!"

"That's it, that's it!" Selene walked halfway down my chest, eagerly nosing the screen. "Hurry up and buy it already."

My phone rang as I put the CyberLitter 5000 in my cart. Clint had written me a check before hurrying to leave my house following the conversation with his brother. The whole confrontation had rattled him, and almost as soon as Seth was gone, so too was Clint.

I glanced over at my phone, ignoring Selene's protests to tune it out and continue the purchase. Leanna's number was on the screen, and for a moment I was glad to have a happy distraction after the emotionally charged evening, but then remembered what day it was. Nearly every Thursday, Leanna tried to coax me into going to Ladies' Night at Merlin's Well. Sometimes I could resist; others I could not. Tonight, I was pretty bushed from dealing with Clint as well as my busy shop. I almost didn't answer, but I didn't want to be rude and send her straight to voicemail.

I pressed the green icon and accepted the call, quickly putting it on speaker. "Hey, you."

"Hey, yourself. Whatcha up to tonight?" Her innocent question belied her mischievous intent. She wanted to lure me out, and while part of me sort of wanted to be lured, I wouldn't let on that I felt that way. Our eternal dance continued.

"Um, buying a fancy litter box for Selene. Have you ever heard of the CyberLitter 5000?"

"Don't those things cost like a fortune?"

"Yes, but I'm not paying for it. Selene managed to extort it out of Clint Bridges."

"Extort?" Selene sputtered. "Extort? How dare you? I earned that money fair and square. I said that I had a spell to let Clint contact his dead brother, and I delivered. It's not my fault his brother had no useful information and was kind of an annoying jerk."

I sighed and rolled my eyes. "You see what I'm dealing with here?"

"Wackiness aside, it sounds to me like Selene has a point. She fulfilled her contractual obligations."

"Exactly." Selene puffed out her chest. "Leanna understands me."

"Yeah? Well, you're free to go move into her loft anytime you want," I muttered in between tapping out my credit card information. I'd never been much of a typist. Hunt and peck was more my speed.

"You'd miss me, and you know it!" Selene insisted.

I finished the shipping information and clicked to the final step of the ordering process. Smiling over at the cat, I said, "At least now I won't have to scoop up after you."

"Oh, like you're a bowl of peaches? Believe me, I've had plenty of mornings where I had to hold off on using my box after you've been in there."

Leanna laughed. "You guys are so funny together, the way you banter."

I bit back a retort about being able to do without Selene's particular kind of "banter."

"I have to find the humor in the situation," Selene said. "After all, my back's always hurting from carrying Cora and her business."

My mouth dropped open. "When's the last time you made a candle? Or counted a till?"

"Those things require opposable thumbs. Would you ask a fish to climb a tree? Besides, you're discounting my invaluable moral support and vast storehouse of knowledge."

"Sounds like you need to ask for a raise, Selene."

"Please, don't encourage her," I groaned.

Leanna giggled. "So, you coming out to the Well tonight or what?"

"I don't know," I said with a sigh. "I'm pretty worn out. I might just hang out and stream something."

"Sounds boring. Come on! You have to come out and protect me. Heather invited Sissy."

"Ugh."

"Tell me about it. But you know Heather. She's just too nice."

"That's what I'm always saying about you, Lee. Heather's just a little less … discerning. In any case, telling me Sissy is going to be there isn't helping your case."

"Come on, please? I need a buffer."

"I don't know … I mean, I don't have anything to wear …"

We both knew I'd already caved and was just going through the motions.

"What about that dark red dress with the flared skirt?"

"The tight one?"

"It's not that tight. I'll see you around eightish."

The call ended and I sighed in defeat.

"Eightish. That's only half an hour before you usually go to bed, right, Cora?"

I turned a glare on the cat. "Do you want me to remove this from my shopping cart and buy a new wardrobe instead? Because that's where we're headed."

"Sure, I'll let you explain to Clint that you spent all of the money on clothes." She paused. "On second thought, he might like that. He does seem to enjoy looking at you."

My cheeks warmed. "Stop it, he does not."

I quickly hit the Order icon, much to Selene's relief, and headed into my bedroom to get dressed. I tried on three different outfits before I caved and tried the red dress. The truth was, it wasn't the tightness that bothered me. It was the dress I'd worn when Roger proposed to me. I'd been avoiding wearing it ever since the divorce.

It was a bit out of style, but not so far as to be overtly obvious. I donned the garment and did something I rarely do: I actually put on cosmetics. Just a thin layer of lip gloss and a bit of eyeshadow and mascara, nothing too heavy. The Well can get pretty packed on Ladies' Night, and that means it can be hot. The last thing I wanted was pancake makeup sliding down my cheeks when it mixed with sweat.

Leanna can wear all the makeup she wants because she never seems to sweat. In fact, there are times I feel clumsy and awkward just being in her presence. She kind of glows, and I, well, I sweat.

I drove to the tavern, lost in thought. The place was packed to the gills, as usual, and it took a few minutes to snag a parking space in the small lot. Once inside, I spotted Leanna at one of the pub tables lining the east wall. She saw me and waved enthusiastically. Sissy and Heather sat at the table as well, and they smiled politely as I approached.

"Woo hoo! Look at the hottie in the red dress," Leanna said, spinning one finger in an attempt to get me to do a twirl.

"Oh, stop," I said, settling in. "How's everyone doing tonight?"

"Great. Lots of good-looking guys in here,"

Leanna said, eying a tall, curly-haired man who strode past.

"I just hope my ex doesn't show up," Heather said with a shudder.

"Speaking of exes," Leanna said, turning to me "how's the whole Roger situation going?"

"Oh sweet Mother Nature, don't ask." I hid my face in my hands. "I ran into him while I was kayaking yesterday and almost capsized."

"Oh dear," Sissy said.

"Well, hopefully he won't show up here tonight," I said. "I've been trying to avoid thinking about him."

"Ooh, look," Sissy said, pointing at the door. "Isn't that Chad?"

Heather yelped and tried to hide behind Leanna. "Oh for crying out loud. Why?"

"Don't worry, he's probably not going to try and talk to you."

"You don't understand," Heather moaned. "He asked me out to dinner a few days ago, after he dropped off the girls. The whole thing was so awkward and I ended up blurting out that I was seeing someone new—which, clearly I am not, but it just sort of popped out of my mouth. If he sees me here alone on singles night, he'll know I was lying."

"Yikes." Leanna frowned. "Well, listen, if he comes over I'll just say I dragged you out tonight."

"That is her MO," I teased.

Leanna flashed a grin. "Oh, come on. Admit it, it's nice to have a night out on the town."

"Any idea why he's suddenly pining to get back together?" Sissy asked, leaning in closer to Heather as if the gossip might somehow slip away if she were any farther back. "Was it more of a hook-up thing, or a real date?"

Heather recoiled slightly from the over-eager woman, but managed to keep a polite smile on her face. "I—I'm not sure. It was sort of out of the blue, but we did have a nice conversation a few weekends ago at Lily's soccer game." Heather paused and twisted her paper cocktail napkin until it was coming apart in her hands. "Oh, I don't know. Should I go over and say hello?"

"Well, is there a chance you might want to get back together with him?" Leanna asked, her tone sympathetic. "I know the divorce is still pretty fresh, but is there a chance that maybe you want to try again?"

"I don't know." Heather gave a nervous shake of her head and then reached for her wine glass. Judging by the look on her face, she was wishing she'd ordered something stronger. "I guess I want to keep my options open. This is my first time being single since I was twenty-one!"

"Speaking of options," Sissy said. "There's that bartender I was telling you guys about. The one Melissa's dead husband was parading all over town."

I followed her gaze to the door and saw a red-haired woman in a tight bodysuit enter the bar. I couldn't tell if she was off-duty, or just about to punch in for her shift.

"She doesn't seem too broken up about his death," Sissy observed. "If that getup doesn't say *I'm available*, I don't know what does."

At some point Heather wandered off with her ex-husband, leaving Sissy to dominate the conversation for the rest of the night. Not that I was surprised. The woman was an ever-flowing fountain of tawdry gossip. Who was sleeping with who seemed the be-all and end-all of her existence. At one point Leanna and I evacuated to the bathroom just to get a break from Gossip Girl.

It was still a couple of hours from last call when I finally gave up and made my excuses for calling it a night. It wasn't just Sissy and her gossiping; I was tired, confused about how I felt with all the recent changes in my life, concerned for poor Clint, and still a bit leery that Roger might show his face.

When I was about ten steps from the exit, the wooden door swung open and Clint appeared. He glanced about and grimaced, not seeing me immediately. I think he was upset at how crowded the place was. He turned on his heel as if to leave, but he noticed me at the last moment.

His eyes widened as he did a double take, glancing over my figure before quickly bringing his gaze back up to mine. He reached up and adjusted his tie.

I smiled as I approached. "Hello."

"Hey." He smiled warmly. "You look really pretty all dressed up."

"Oh. Thank you." I hoped the low lighting in the bar concealed my flushed cheeks.

Clint looked past me at the packed bar. "I think I'm going to get going. I know I just got here, but …"

"What's wrong?"

"Most of the people in town still think I'm a cold-blooded killer. I thought maybe I could just duck in here for a couple of quick drinks, and not be recognized, but …"

"You picked the wrong night, I'm afraid. It's

Ladies' Night, and the Well is always packed on Ladies' Night."

"I was just going nuts in my hotel room, you know? I needed some air. A distraction. Even with the TV on, it's just not enough." He started to say something else, but thought better of it and shook it away.

I nodded. "That's understandable. It's been a rough night." The redheaded bartender strolled past us, now wearing an apron around her curvy hips as she took orders and chatted with the patrons. I gestured toward her. "Do you recognize her?"

He followed my gaze. "No. Should I?"

"That's the woman your brother Seth was having an affair with."

Clint's jaw worked silently as he glared at her. "I think we should go talk to her."

Before I could say anything, he strode purposefully across the bar. I followed Clint a pace behind, struggling to catch up as he confronted her.

"Excuse me, Miss," he said. "I would like to have a word with you."

Her eyes ran up and down Clint. "I know you, you're Seth's brother. Clint."

"Is it true then? Were you having an affair with my brother?"

"I'm not sure that it's any of your business, but yes. Technically speaking. He told me he was separated. I only just found out that wasn't the case." The woman tucked her chin for a moment. "He told me he was getting a divorce soon, and that after the paperwork was done, we could take things to the next level."

Clint softened a little. "I see."

"I didn't know his wife was pregnant, either," she added. "Your brother was a good liar."

"I'm sorry that happened to you," Clint told her. "Believe me, I'm under no illusion that Seth was a saint."

The woman scoffed. "No. I guess at least I know I'm not the only one he was screwing. Have you talked to his business partner since all of this happened? Anderson something or other."

Clint frowned. "Anderson Millwright?"

"Yeah, that's the guy. Apparently, Anderson thought Seth was lazy and didn't pull his weight. There were quite a few times they fought about it. Sometimes Seth would yell at him over the phone, and vice versa, right in front of me. Like I wanted to deal with that." She sniffed in disgust.

"So things were bad between them?" I asked.

"You could say that. Seth was upset because his

partner was trying to push him out. He wanted to buy him out so he could bring in a new partner. What he didn't know was that Seth was trying to do the same thing." The woman shook her head. "I guess I dodged a bullet. If you'll excuse me, I have a lot of orders to fill."

I exchanged glances with Clint. "Thank you for your time."

We left her and headed for the exit. I noticed Leanna, Heather, and Sissy watching us intently from the corner table.

"Oh great," I muttered. "I'm going to have a LOT of explaining to do."

12

*T*he stars shone overhead in a brilliant celestial tapestry as I drove home. I'd only had a single glass of wine over the span of the three hours I'd stayed at the tavern, listening to Sissy blabber on. After I left the bar with Clint, he'd offered to take me somewhere else for a nightcap, but I'd turned him down. It was late and my mind felt more than a little fried. He'd walked me to my car and we said goodnight. The attraction and chemistry were still there, smoldering beneath the surface, but the conversation he'd had with his brother had dashed the sparks I'd felt growing during our impromptu dinner at my kitchen table. Was a romance even possible in the midst of such a heavy and emotionally charged situation? And even if it was, was it what I wanted?

I honestly didn't know. A week ago, when Clint had been just a handsome stranger, a customer in my shop, the possibility of a romance had thrilled me. But now, the idea was wrapped in layers of complications, and I wasn't sure how we'd manage to untangle them.

It was hard to think about Clint without thinking of the terrible murder itself. Seth didn't know who'd killed him. He couldn't even remember lighting my candle. However, he had been quick to accuse Clint of his murder. There was clearly no love lost between the brothers.

Sibling rivalry didn't mean murder, though. More and more, a picture was emerging of Seth Bridges, and it was not a very flattering one. Cheating on his wife, sloughing off the workload onto his business partner while simultaneously trying to cheat him out of the business they'd built together. And the things he'd said about Clint … unforgivable. He wasn't the type of man I could feel a lot of sympathy for, but that didn't mean he'd deserved death.

What it did mean was that there were more than a few people who might have wanted him dead. Men like that, who plowed through life with little to no regard for others, usually weren't short on enemies and critics. In fact, I was starting to wonder if his business partner could have done the deed. It certainly sounded like he had motivation to do so. I didn't know him personally, however, and decided to reserve judgment until I could find out more. Both about him, and his situation with Seth.

When I pulled up in front of my house, I was no closer to finding mental solace. I almost looked forward to bantering with Selene just as a distraction from my myriad troubles. That's when I knew I'd hit a low point.

I exited the car and strode up the driveway to my front porch. Tiny sprites glowed like golden fireflies in the night and drew a smile from me, despite my heavy thoughts. One of them alighted on a long blade of grass, silhouetting itself against its own light.

I fumbled with the keys, then pushed the front door open. I flipped on lights and looked about for Selene, but she didn't seem to be around. "Selene? Are you home?"

No response. I waited several more moments before calling out again, and got the same results.

"You'd better not be hiding somewhere ready to leap out at me."

Just to be on the safe side, I filled her food dish as my first priority, checked her water and its filter, and then sidled off to my bedroom to change clothes. I'd been done wearing this dress hours ago, and the heels weren't helping either.

My eyes ached for sleep, looking puffy and swollen in the bathroom mirror. I stifled a yawn, and quickly removed my makeup before shuffling off to bed. I crashed onto the mattress and pulled a light sheet over my body. My eyes closed, my body stilled, yet I couldn't quiet my racing mind.

Keeping my eyes shut only served to provide a blank canvas for my imagination to weave its own tales. I had visions of Clint holding a bloody silver candelabra, and then of Roger joining him and laughing for some reason. Not real visions—that wasn't a part of my magical gifts—just the musings of an exhausted mind cursed to find no slumber.

I opened my eyes and watched the silver moonbeams move across the walls and ceiling as the night wore on. I finally threw my sheet off and rose from my bed, deciding to no longer fight a battle I was doomed to lose.

Selene still hadn't returned home. I put on a pair

of shorts and a tank top and went to the kitchen. The lights seemed bright to my tired eyes. I put on a kettle of water for tea and tuned up my relaxing playlist, using Bluetooth to stream it through the soundbar hanging under the flatscreen television I rarely had time to watch.

While John Legend crooned out "Conversations in the Dark," I steeped my tea and extricated my journal. Just the act of getting it out and opening it to a fresh page helped me sort out my thinking.

I went out tonight with Leanna and Heather. Sissy was there, too, and dominated the conversation as usual. I couldn't stop watching the door, because I was afraid Roger would come in.

I looked at the page and sighed. Am I really that whiny?

I don't know what to think about Roger. Part of me wants him to stay away because he complicates my life, but I'll admit some of me is glad he came back to town. Does he regret what happened? Or did he just run home after he lost his job in New York City? Maybe it has nothing to do with me.

I doodled in the side margin while my mind wandered. I sipped some of the tea and added a smidge more milk. Clint sprang into my mind, and I once again put pen to paper.

Clint showed up at Merlin's Well right when I was about to leave. I just looked up and there he was. Looking miserable. I think he wanted to get his drink on in private, but he made the mistake of hitting up the Well on Ladies' Night. He went and talked to his dead brother's former mistress. I didn't get her name. Really kind of an ice queen if you ask me. Clint pressed her for information, and she confirmed that Seth was having problems with his business partner.

I considered the page for a moment and wrote the word "suspects" large, using two lines. Then I made bullet points and put down names. Anderson Millwright. Bartender? Then, with great reluctance, I wrote down Clint's name as well.

Under their names, I wrote down little notes that might implicate them in the crime. It didn't sit right to be treating Clint that way, though, and I had trouble concentrating.

I took a break from journaling about Roger, Clint, and the murder to concentrate on my Aunt Lavender. She'd disappeared so many times before, I suppose I'd just gotten used to it. Tonight, though, I found my thoughts leaning in a different direction.

I'm worried about Aunt Lavender. I don't know why. Everyone keeps telling me it's no big deal. It's hardly out of character for her to disappear like this, sometimes for even longer periods of time. But still, something about it feels wrong this time. I wish she'd just give in and get a cell phone. A woman her age ...

I scratched out the last sentence and started anew.

I guess I never worried about Aunt Lavender before. I worried plenty that she'd forget to show up for a magical lesson or to come to a swim meet. I worried about her missing my birthday. I just never worried about her safety before, because she always seemed invincible.

I read somewhere once that childhood ends the moment you learn you're going to die. I respectfully disagree. Childhood ends the day you look at your parents and mentors and realize they're only human, too. Well, witches in this case, but still, the point stands.

Thinking of Lavender as vulnerable, and maybe in trouble, was something new to me. I recalled that photo she kept, in one of the few clear spots in her house. The one with me and Evan in it. It wasn't a big, sweeping gesture, but in all the mess and chaos that was Lavender's house, it was the only personal photo I'd ever seen there before.

I laid my pen down and closed the journal. I picked up my cell to skip a song and noticed it wasn't as late as I'd thought. There was a good chance my mom was still awake.

I found myself calling her before I'd really consciously made the decision. She'd said she would try to find Lavender with her scrying mirror. Maybe she'd already found out where she was and had forgotten to call and let me know.

"Cora?" My mother's voice didn't have the thickness of sleep, so I figured I was right and she'd yet to retire for the evening. "You're up late."

"Yeah, I couldn't sleep." I rubbed my eyes with the heels of my hands. "Selene's still gone, and the house is empty, and I guess I'm worried about Aunt Lavender."

"I see." Mom's voice had that kind of lilt you hear when someone has bad news and doesn't want to tell you. I hated to ask the question that next spilled from my lips, because I felt I already knew the answer.

"Did you happen to find Aunt Lavender with the scrying mirror?"

Mom hesitated a moment before answering. "No, I didn't."

Even though I'd been expecting the news, it still hit me like a gut punch. I sighed and leaned back in my chair.

"That doesn't mean she's not alive and well, dear," Mom said hastily. "There are a lot of reasons why the scrying mirror might not work. She could be in the Faerie Realm, or in a cavern filled with dragon stone, or any number of things."

"Who are you trying to convince, Mom? Me, or yourself."

Mom heaved a long sigh. "Can it be both?"

"Yes, it certainly can be both." I pursed my lips, wishing my mother could have made herself sound more convincing. I almost told her about Aunt Lavender leaving so much of her normal equipment behind for this jaunt, but I decided to keep it to myself. Mom was already worried, and the last thing I wanted to do was heap more problems onto her shoulders. The two sisters were somewhat estranged, thanks to years of missed obligations and hurt feelings, but I never doubted she loved Lavender.

"I don't know what to say, really." Mom's voice held a note of self-recrimination. "Your Aunt Lavender has been in more places than Johnny Cash. I almost feel silly worrying about her at all."

"I know what you mean. It's hard to imagine Aunt Lavender in trouble."

"Yeah, she usually starts the trouble," Mom said.

We shared a laugh, tinged with a bit of melancholy. It occurred to me that we both missed Lavender in our own ways. I guess maybe we just got so used to the idea of her always coming back from her wild adventures in one piece we kind of took her for granted.

"I hope she's all right," I said as our laughter wound down.

"Me, too."

"Well, if you hear anything about Aunt Lavender—"

"I'll be sure to let you know. Love you, Cora."

"Love you too, Mom."

I ended the call and sighed. I still didn't feel like sleeping. I slipped on a pair of sweats over my shorts, grabbed my keys, and headed out to Aunt Lavender's house.

At night, it seemed foreboding. The graying paint appeared as ebon black, as if it were a house of horrors rather than a charming bungalow. The trees flanking her house took on a sinister cast, their branches becoming skeletal fingers rasping at the siding as if seeking entry to suck the life out of those who dwelt within.

I suppressed a shudder. *What would I have to*

worry about in a haunted house, anyway? I'm a witch, right? Haunted houses should be ho-hum.

I couldn't shake the feeling that something was amiss, even as I knocked on the front door a single time and the house allowed me entry. I pushed inside and flipped on the lights. The house seemed a lot less creepy with the lights on, that was for certain.

I sidled through the corridors formed by her hoarded treasures, searching for a clue to her where-abouts. Along the way I stopped to fix a tumble of paperback books that had fallen across the path.

I tried looking in drawers for Aunt Lavender's journal but couldn't find it. I did find a drawer full of different lengths of wire, a cupboard stuffed to the gills with Russian dolls of all colors and models, and every Bee Gees album known to man.

I settled into one of the few empty chairs and sighed. Nothing. It was as if Aunt Lavender had simply vanished into thin air. Here today, gone tomorrow. All we are is just dust in the wind …

A hard thump caused my heart to skip a beat. I looked up at the ceiling. Aunt Lavender's bungalow didn't have a second floor, but it did have a walk-in —make that climb-in—attic.

I was not alone. Someone was in the house with me.

13

I glanced up at the ceiling warily as I waited to hear another sound from the attic. For long, tense moments all I could hear was the sound of my own heartbeat pounding in my veins. I tried to quiet my breathing, afraid it would alert the intruder to my presence.

Cold fear gripped my belly. What if they'd already been alerted to my presence? I'd certainly made no effort to be stealthy. Perhaps they saw the lights go on. Were they up there, waiting to pounce? Or waiting for me to leave?

Barely daring to breathe, I stared at the ceiling and waited.

I heard another hard thump, then a series of smaller ones. As if something had been dislodged and rolled across the floor, like a bottle or a jar. Deciding I couldn't sit there any longer, I rose carefully from the chair, wincing as its aged timber creaked.

At first I thought to head out the front door and escape. Then, something hardened within me. I decided not to surrender one square foot of territory to the intruder. After all, I was far from helpless. Defensive spells weren't my forte, but I wasn't completely inept at them either.

At least, that's what I told myself while steeling my nerves. It took a great deal of effort to turn away from the front door and head toward the attic stairs, but I did it.

I walked under the pull string, and realized I'd have to move a stack of empty picture frames if I wanted to deploy the ladder. Which also raised the question as to how the intruder had gotten up there. As quietly as I could manage, I moved the frames to the side.

When a small patch of space was cleared, I reached up and grabbed the pull string, giving it a hard yank. The ceiling panel dropped down, revealing the folded ladder behind it. The ladder unfolded smoothy as I guided it with my hands until the feet rested firmly on the floor.

I stared up into the dark hole of the attic. It seemed like the yawning maw of some fell beast intent upon devouring me. "Okay, Cora, get a grip," I whispered to myself. I backtracked a step and hit the light switch in the hallway. Nothing happened. The hole remained dark.

"Of course," I muttered. I cast a minor spell that created a tiny orb of light, and I slowly ascended the stairs. When I reached the top, I summoned a mini cyclone and kept it spinning in my palm.

Aunt Lavender's attic proved to be just as over-stuffed as the rest of her house. I saw a menacing group of figures and nearly hurled my cyclone until I realized it was just a collection of child-sized dress mannequins. That's pretty creepy, Aunt Lavender. Real creepy.

It got worse as I probed deeper into the attic's dusty, cramped environs. I came across a collection of clown marionettes that gave the mannequins a run for their money on the bone-chilling scale. Their beady black painted eyes seemed to follow me as I went. I kept the cyclone going in my hand as a kind of security blanket.

I came across an empty mason jar lying on the wooden timbers of the attic floor. One of the old ones, made of glass so thick and green you could not see very well through it. I began to doubt myself. Maybe the jar had fallen and rolled across the floor on its own. That wasn't out of the realm of reasonable possibilities, was it?

Still, I felt as if there had to be someone … or some*thing*. My naked eyes belied that notion, but I could feel a presence in the room. I completed my sweep of the attic, or at least the places a human body could fit, even with contortion, then replaced the mason jar in its spot and grunted at my own foolishness. I extinguished the orb of light and the cyclone of wind, admonishing myself for my own paranoia, then headed for the ladder.

A dark shape leaped out of the shadows at me. "BOO!"

I shrieked and fell over a stack of Styrofoam egg crates in my efforts to escape. I became aware of feline laughter, which is felt more than heard. Selene leaped up onto a crate and peered down at me with her azure-eyed gaze.

"Ha! You should see your face. Did you pee yourself? Tell me that you peed yourself, because that would really put a cherry on it for me."

"Selene?" I sat up in a huff. "What are you doing skulking around Lavender's attic in the middle of the night?"

"I could ask you why you're skulking around the main floor in the middle of the night."

"I wasn't skulking!" I gasped in exasperation. "I mean, come on. I was searching."

"Well, so was I. I was also searching."

"For what?"

Selene's ears went back, and her head drooped toward the floor. "I was looking for clues as to where Lavender might have gotten off to. Same as you, I'd imagine."

I was not used to the acerbic cat being sincere. I wasn't sure I liked the implications. As long as Selene was making wisecracks and trying to make my life miserable, it was like a sign from the Mother that all was well with the universe. I felt justified in my worry for Lavender like never before.

"When *was* the last time you saw Lavender, Selene?" I asked softly.

"I told you. It was only a day or two before I came to live with you." Selene looked out the tiny attic window, tail swishing slowly. It was open, explaining her access to the stifling room. "We were having dinner," she said after a long moment. "Lavender was all over the place, jabbering on, unable to stay focused on one topic for more than a few minutes at a time. It's how she always gets right before she leaves on one of her jaunts."

I nodded. I knew that behavior. Lavender's flighty tendencies increased tenfold when she was planning an adventure. She rushed about her home like mad, gathering supplies, collecting notes, and babbling on incessantly about whatever her latest obsession was. One month it would be a search for the Sword of Damascus, the next the hanging gardens of Babylon. It seemed like Lavender always had a new quest, a new frontier to be explored.

I was the wind witch in the family, yet she often acted like a tornado. And it was best to stand back and stay out of her way while she rampaged through life. When I'd been younger, I'd begged Lavender to take me with her. She'd always refused, telling me "Maybe next time." After a while I stopped asking, because "next time" never came.

"So she *was* about to go on one of her adventures, then. That means she could be back any day now."

"I don't know." Selene's tail twitched in agitation. "In hindsight, she never mentioned going on an excursion. Then there's the fact that she left so many of her staples behind. It's not like her, even at her most frenzied."

I wiped the sweat off my brow and sighed. "Tell

you what, let's continue this discussion downstairs. This attic is too hot for me to think clearly."

We convened down in the kitchen. I took the liberty to brew a cup of tea on the stove while Selene continued her tale.

"I asked Lavender if she was planning a trip. She told me no." Selene's ears went back. "She told me no, but when I woke up the next day, she was gone. She'd never lied to me like that before, not in our sixteen years together."

Selene slumped, her head and tail pointed toward the floor. For only the second time since meeting her, I felt an actual stab of sympathy for the cat.

"Maybe she had a good reason for not telling you what was going on?"

"Like what?" Selene looked up at me sullenly. "What possible reason could she have had to keep me in the dark?"

"Well …" I cleared my throat awkwardly. "Uh. Well, what if she were trying to protect you?"

"From what? Since when has Lavender ever really taken the time to think about someone other than herself, anyway?"

I was surprised by the bitterness in Selene's tone. It mirrored that which dwelt within my own chest any time the subject of Aunt Lavender came up.

It struck me that the cat felt abandoned. Perhaps every bit as abandoned as I had when Lavender would forget about a promise she made to me. It stung. Even though I knew she didn't mean to hurt me, it did.

"There must be something we're missing. Some clue. What had she been working on? She always gathers a bunch of books and texts when she's plotting something."

"She'd been shutting me out of her work," Selene admitted. "Keeping doors closed so I couldn't get inside and see what she was reading. It wasn't like her, but then, we'd been having our own relationship trials as of late."

"You never told me that part," I said softly.

"I told you why I came to live with you. I told you what happened when she left me behind the last time. It was awful! I thought I would die. All I could do was lie around and feel my magic drain away little by little." The cat shuddered. "I've served the Hearth family for generations. I'm bound to the family line. Normally, I don't join a new witch until the old one passes."

"Right." I nodded. "You did tell me that part, though if I'm being honest, I'm still not sure how it works. How the binding rituals we did were able to take effect while your previous guardian was still alive."

A new and terrible thought struck me like a bite from a snake.

"Unless ..."

Selene's eyes flashed cold as ice. "Don't even say it. Lavender isn't dead. I just took matters into my own paws. That's all," she hissed. "I knew you were boring as heck, but I also knew you were one thing Lavender could never be: reliable."

I bristled. The word didn't sound like a compliment, but Selene was in a foul mood. I wasn't going to push her buttons further.

"Okay," I said, exhaling slowly. "Well, let's try to find her ... together."

Selene seemed to relax a bit. "Okay. Together, then. Two heads are better than one—though I fail to see how your candle-making skills are going to be of much use."

I clenched my teeth to repress a comeback. "What do you want to do now?" I asked.

"Let's divide the house into quadrants and do a grid search. There has to be *something* here that will give us a clue as to where she might have gotten off to, right?"

"Right."

"At least you have opposable thumbs," Selene muttered, striding down the hallway toward the back bedrooms.

I opened all of the doors and we moved through the cramped environs of her house, searching high and low—me being high, her being low—for any signs Lavender might have left that would clue us in to her destination.

I rummaged through boxes, emptied out drawers, and dug into her closets in search of evidence, yet came up with nothing time and time again. Judging by the way Selene muttered and hissed as she rummaged around on her level, I assumed her efforts were met with a similar lack of success.

"This is hopeless!" Selene bounded up to the top of the *National Geographic* magazine stacks and glared about. "I don't know what we were expecting. A note? Ha! Lavender couldn't plan far enough ahead to compose a note."

"Well, I don't see any sign of where she went, but let's look at the bright side." I looked about us and shook my head. "We also haven't found any signs of foul play. That's good, right?"

"The absence of evidence is not evidence of absence," Selene said.

"I am way too tired to try and make sense of that right now," I said through a barely stifled yawn.

Selene looked around. "I suppose we should call it a night."

I knew it was well into the small hours of the morning, but I was afraid to check my phone. "Agreed. I have to restock the shop to get ready for Saturday's rush. It's one of the last weekends of summer, which means it will be busy."

"Then let's go home," Selene said. I felt a slight rush of warmth at the way she called my house home. I started to go to the front door, but then I was struck with an idea.

"Wait a minute, Selene. We can't leave yet."

"Why not?"

"We need to gather some personal items of Lavender's. A comb or brush would be ideal; so would any jewelry or necklaces she might have favored. Pretty much anything she spent a lot of time with."

"You want to try a divination spell?" Selene asked.

"No, I want my mom to try a divination spell."

Selene seemed pleased. "That's a good idea. Lavender mentioned that your mother is good at divination magic. Excels at it even."

"Not to mention the fact that she's Lavender's little sister. That kind of familial bond helps strengthen the magic."

I found a hairbrush in the bathroom, still tangled with some of her wavy, graying tresses. Selene directed me to Lavender's jewelry box and pointed out a ring Lavender liked to wear on special occasions, and lastly, I took along her favorite mortar and pestle. She'd probably spent more time holding it than all the other things combined.

Once we were loaded up on trinkets to help Mom cast the divination spell, Selene and I took our leave. I cast one last glance at the black house, and felt a stab of the emptiness left behind by Lavender.

Then I turned my eyes to the road and drove home in silence.

14

Selene and I dropped the items off at my mom's house the following morning, offering a rushed explanation before piling back into the car and driving to Wicked Wicks just in time to open for the day.

The weekend passed without any word from either my mother in regard to the divination efforts, or from Clint about the murder investigation. I fell back into my old routines, albeit with a bit more moodiness. I created candles in the shop, fighting the never-ending battle against depleted stock. I got in a round of kayaking after work on Sunday evening, and managed to catch up on a little bit of reading at night.

I journaled, I ate and slept, but through it all

pervaded a sense of sinister anticipation. I awaited both good news and bad. Schrödinger's anticipation, I suppose. Even as I hoped to hear news of Aunt Lavender in good health, I dreaded to hear of some tragedy befalling her. Likewise, I awaited news on the criminal case. While I could be hopeful of hearing news that would exonerate Clint, I also dreaded evidence that would condemn him as a murderer.

My mind played tricks on me. On Monday morning, I was awoken in the wee hours with the panicked notion that Clint had been arrested and taken into custody. It would explain why he hadn't come around in several days, if nothing else.

I opened my shop and settled in for a busy day. I flitted between my workstation and helping the patrons who wandered in my door. Selene seemed oddly subdued and kept her verbal barbs to a bare minimum. I was starting to worry about her.

After returning from a rushed lunch break, I was working to get back into the flow when the brass bell hanging above the entrance rang. "Welcome," I called without looking up from my work. When no one replied, I glanced up and gasped in surprise. "Roger?"

"Hello, again." Roger's handsome face was cleanly

shaven, his skin smooth and tight. He smelled of just the right amount of cologne, not like some guys who take a bath in the stuff. In addition, he wore a light green check patterned tie over a charcoal shirt tailored to his athletically slim form for a flattering fit. He looked like a male fashion model in a magazine ad who had just stepped off the page. "You look great, Cora."

I felt a flush come to my cheeks and dropped my gaze to the counter. "Thank you."

Roger glanced down at the take-out cup holder in his hands. Two drink cups were situated on one side, while a pastry bag sat in the other two cups. "I come bearing gifts," he said.

He set the cardboard drink holder on the counter and I breathed a sigh of relief at the sight of the Dragon's Gold Coffee logo on the side. At least he'd remembered to steer clear of poor Julia next door.

"What's this for?" I asked.

His dark eyes glowed with delight as he set aside the pastry bag, which emanated a wonderful aroma. "Just thought you might need a Monday afternoon pick-me-up. I imagine you had a busy weekend. I drove by yesterday and it looked like you had a packed house."

I smiled. "It was pretty nuts." I reached for one of the cups, but Roger redirected me to the other one.

"That one is yours." He gestured at the cluttered workstation. "Business is booming; why not hire a permanent employee to help ease your burden?"

I took a sip of the coffee and found he remembered my favorite drink. Warm vanilla and brown sugar rolled over my tongue in a sea of frothy oat milk and espresso. "I probably should," I replied after that first swallow. "It has been super busy all summer. Although, as they say, hard on the feet, easy on the bottom line."

Roger laughed. "I suppose that's one way of looking at things."

"Is that for me, too?" I asked, grinning at the pastry bag.

"Indeed it is," Roger replied with a grin of his own. He pulled the bag open and my smile widened even further at the sight of a chocolate dragon hoard cookie—a signature creation from the independent coffee house. Think chocolate chip cookies with some extra amenities, like toffee and peanut butter chips. I don't know the exact recipe, and I'm loath to learn it, because I enjoy the mystery.

"I take it you're still into these cookies," Roger said with a chuckle as he watched my eyes light up.

I snatched the cookie from the bag, broke it in half, losing a few crumbled chunks in the process, before extending the second half toward him. "If you're trying to score points, you're batting a thousand. But here, if I eat this whole thing, I swear I'll gain five pounds."

He chuckled, but his eyes grew serious. "It wouldn't matter if you did. You're just as beautiful as the day we met, out there on the lake."

I popped a bite of cookie in my mouth to stall for time.

Roger leaned in a little closer, ignoring his own piece of cookie. "The truth is, Cora, I haven't been able to get you out of my mind since I came back to town."

My heart skipped a beat before it dove headfirst into familiar—yet frightening—territory. Roger wasn't just some guy trying to ply me with gifts. He was so much more than that, which was both incredibly tempting and repelling, somehow in equal measure.

"I'd like to take you to dinner, Cora. One dinner. If you hate it, I swear, I'll never bring it up again."

I looked into his eyes. Soulful, pleading. I couldn't help but wonder "what if?"

This is the Roger I fell in love with. Attentive.

Thoughtful. Focused on me, caring about me. I missed this Roger so very much ...

"Roger ..." I heaved a sigh. "I don't know if that's such a good idea."

"Why not?" His voice wasn't petulant, or indignant. Just questioning, and a bit hurt.

"Look, it's the first time we've really seen each other since the divorce. I'm not sure we should just go pole vaulting into anything."

"It's not pole vaulting," Roger laughed. I'd missed his laugh as well. "It's just dinner."

I looked at him askance. "Roger, given our history, there's no way in heck you can convince me that this is 'just dinner.' Not in a million years."

"At least he had the good sense to ditch that ridiculous mustache," Selene quipped from behind me.

I jolted, having completely forgotten she'd come to the shop with me that morning.

"What happened?" she continued. "Did the '70s call and demand it back?"

Roger cocked an eyebrow at Selene, unsure if he wanted to be amused or insulted.

"We all know you're after more than just a little dinner," Selene added. "Let's examine the evidence. Exhibit A: Your freshly shaven face. Cora didn't like the mustache, so you ditched it. Exhibit B. You brought an admitted bribe along, hoping to take advantage of the endorphins running through poor Cora's brain while she ate her favorite cookie and drank her favorite coffee."

"*Poor Cora?*" I repeated with a scowl. "Selene, I'm not some kind of child who gets a sugar high and forgets how to act. Besides, it's a latte, not a love potion."

Selene ignored me and continued presenting her case, "Exhibit C: You, in a suit? Who are you kidding?"

"He looks good, Selene," I said, feeling the need to come to Roger's rescue.

"I'm not disputing that for an oaf, he cuts a good figure. My point is, Roger's not a suit guy. He's a flannel shirt and blue jeans kind of guy. I think he felt a bit self-conscious because that Clint fellow was outdressing him."

"Selene, you barely know him," I argued, though she had something of a point. Was he going to a job interview after this or something?

Roger's cheeks turned a bit crimson, and he laughed helplessly. "All right, all right. I admit I was looking for more than 'just dinner' when I came in the door—"

My phone rang. Not the shop phone, my personal cell. I glanced at the screen and noticed it was Clint calling.

My heart sputtered. I hadn't heard from him in days and was eager to hear if there was news with the murder investigation. "I have to take this."

Roger stood by awkwardly while I picked up the phone and turned my back on the shop. "Clint? Where have you been? I was worried sick. I thought maybe you'd been arrested or something."

"I'm sorry about that, Cora." His voice sounded heavy. "I've been trying to follow up on our leads."

"Have you found anything?" I walked over toward the rear wall of shelves behind the counter.

"Not really, I'm afraid." He heaved a sigh. "So far, I still look like the prime suspect. But I did find out that Anderson Millwright is still in Winterspell."

"He is? I would have thought he'd have been all fired up to take control of the business by himself."

"Oh, I'm sure that he is, but he wants to stay for the funeral from what I understand." He cleared his throat. "Actually, that's why I was calling you, Cora."

"Oh?"

"Yes. You see, I know which hotel Anderson's staying at, and I'd like to talk to him about Seth, the murder, the affair. Everything."

"What do you need me for? I don't even know the guy. I mean, no offense, you know I'd be happy to help. I'm just a little unclear as to what I can do."

"I want you there, just in case he says something relevant to the case or makes a slip. That way I have a, well, a neutral third party as a witness. You know?"

Clint seemed pretty anxious about the whole thing. Then again, I suppose I would be anxious too, were I accused of murdering my own brother and was about to speak to someone who might have been able to exonerate me.

"All right, Clint. I'll tag along. Where is he staying?"

"The Winterspell Chalet. Do you know where it's at?"

"The Chalet?" I whistled. "Man, at least he knows how to stay in style."

"I'll take that as a yes. Can you meet me there in an hour?"

"I don't close for two."

"Two hours, then?"

"Yeah, that should be doable."

"Thanks. I owe you one, Cora."

The call ended and I turned back around. "Sorry, Roger. I didn't mean to ..."

My voice trailed off. I was talking to empty air. Roger was nowhere to be seen, but his steaming coffee cup and half a broken cookie still rested on the sales counter.

FOR THE REST of the day, I thought about calling Roger, but just as I'd reach for the phone, a rush of customers would sweep through the door. By the time I got a chance to breathe, it was nearly closing time.

I shooed the last customer out the door ten minutes after my official closing time, did a hasty sweep, and then counted my till. I stashed the deposit in the floor safe, since I was running late, and drove to the Chalet.

Calling the Chalet a hotel is like calling the crown jewels a collection of baubles. The Winterspell Chalet straddles the line between upscale hotel and top tier luxury ski lodge. Not to mention the Icefire day spa, which rests upon its grounds.

Mom jokes that the Chalet will just continuously expand until it takes up the entire town, but she's being hyperbolic. The truth is, the Chalet is pretty satisfied with their current market share. And why wouldn't they be? Even in slow times for tourism, they can still make money by renting out their banquet hall and convention rooms.

The Chalet has a warm and rustic elegance to it. Lots of dark, polished wood and leather. I liked the effect. There's nothing better after having been on the blinding white slopes all day than coming to a warm, dark environment. Gave the old eyeballs a rest.

I pushed through the foyer of the Chalet and strode across the thin carpet stretching from entrance to front desk. I spotted Clint nearby, sitting in the lounge. He stood up quickly and came to my side.

"Cora," he said, smiling though I could tell he was anxious to speak to Anderson. "Thank you for coming."

"Yeah, of course. Is he in?"

"Anderson? I was just about to check."

We walked up to the front desk and inquired about Anderson's room. The clerk couldn't tell us the room number, because of privacy laws, but he offered to contact Anderson and see if he wanted to meet us in the lobby.

We settled down to wait. Clint kept glancing anxiously at the steps leading down from the second story. Just when I was about to suggest that Anderson had decided against speaking with us, a man in a suit came down the steps to the lobby, glancing around in that awkward, blind-date sort of way.

I nudged Clint with my elbow and he jumped up from the leather sofa like it was spring-loaded with an ejection seat. He hurried over to the man and introduced himself. "Anderson Millwright?"

The man nodded. He was probably a solid decade older than Clint, with the beginning of middle-aged spread. His mustache and beard were salt and pepper speckled. The light shone off a bald pate that had clearly been waxed. At least he had an attractive bald head. Believe me, I've seen more than a few that weren't. Although, oddly enough, that seemed to be a new habit I'd picked up. I blamed Selene. She loved to people watch from the front window all day, commenting on little things like that.

Anderson and Clint exchanged a handshake. "You're Seth's brother, right?"

"Right. Clint. And this is my friend, Cora."

Anderson offered me his hand and I took it with a polite smile.

"It's nice to meet you," Clint said, gesturing toward a cluster of wooden tables on the other side of the lobby from the sofa we'd been sitting on.

"Nice to meet you, too," Anderson replied. "Though I wish it were under better circumstances." His lips twisted into a frown. "What did you want to speak to me about?"

"We heard that you had something of a heated argument with Seth the night he died," I said by way of breaking the ice. Anderson flinched a little, but he didn't seem especially scared or put off.

"Yes, I was at Seth's house that night, as a matter of fact. Something I told the police, I might add. I didn't kill your brother, Clint, if that's what you're insinuating."

"We're not insinuating anything," Clint said quickly. "We just wanted to get a clearer picture of what happened."

Anderson sighed, his eyes seeming haunted. "I did have an argument with Seth that night. It got pretty bad. I said some things … some things that I wish I could take back. If I'd known that it would be the last time that I spoke to Seth, well …"

"We're all feeling regret, Mr. Millwright," Clint said.

"The police suspected me too, you know,"

Anderson said. "They questioned me for hours, took my prints, the whole nine yards. I guess I'm lucky they didn't find my prints on the murder weapon."

"I didn't kill my brother," Clint said firmly. "My fingerprints were on the candelabra because I'd given it to my mother that night, as a gift. I'm still a little foggy on the details of how it even wound up at my brother and sister-in-law's home."

Anderson considered Clint for a moment, and it felt like he was trying to run him through some kind of mental lie detector test. He must have passed, because after a moment, Anderson inclined his head. "I really don't know much about the investigation. The police told me I was free to leave, but I thought I would stick around and attend the funeral. Your brother and I had our differences, but we went through a lot together. There's a history there. I'd like a chance to say goodbye."

Clint nodded. "I don't think anyone will object to that."

"Anderson, you probably knew him better than most," I interjected. "Can you think of anyone who would want to kill him?"

The question hung heavy in the air like the oppressive heat right before a mountain storm.

"No," Anderson said, shaking his bald head. "I

can't think of anyone who would consider him a true enemy. Although, he was running low on actual friends."

Clint frowned. "What do you mean?"

Anderson looked like he regretted making the off the cuff remark. But he sighed and answered Clint's question. "Seth was sort of alienating his friends here in Winterspell. Spends all his time with the 'wife.'"

Anderson made air quotes when he said the last word.

"I'm sorry, I don't understand the quotes." Clint's eyes narrowed with suspicion.

"Nothing. I've probably already said too much."

"Come on. You can't say something like that and then just leave it."

Anderson heaved a sigh. "Your brother's marriage to that Melissa woman is a sham."

"You mean they have a bad marriage?"

"No, I mean the marriage itself is a sham. A fake. Seth told everyone they eloped and took a bunch of photos barefoot on the beach, under an arch of flowers. The truth is, it's just a business arrangement."

"How do you know all of this?" Clint demanded. "I don't know any of this and Seth was my brother."

"A few weeks back, Seth was depressed. He flew

down to my place in Santa Barbara. We went out for a few drinks, and Seth got wasted. I mean, completely hammered. He started confessing the whole thing to me. He actually cares for this woman, she's some long-time crush, but no matter what he does she won't give him the kind of real relationship he wants ... or I should say, wanted. Past tense now, I suppose."

"What did you say to that?"

"He didn't last too long after that, passed out on my couch, and by the time he sobered up the next day, he didn't want to talk about it. Clammed right up."

Clint and I exchanged looks. "Thank you for your time, Mr. Millwright."

We left the hotel, with more questions than answers.

15

"Well, now what?" I turned to Clint, using my hand to shield my eyes from the red-gold light of the sun as it dropped low enough to kiss the surrounding mountain range.

"I don't know," he confessed. "I can't believe what Anderson Millwright said about my brother."

"That his marriage was a sham?" I pursed my lips in thought. In theory, I understood the concept of fighting with one's siblings over the family purse, but I had no idea what that would actually feel like. My family wasn't poor, but the Bridges had generational wealth. I was curious just how much money was on the line, but couldn't figure out a polite way to ask for even a ballpark number.

"Yeah. I just don't get it. Why lie about something

like that?" Clint scratched behind his head. "Unless Seth was lying to Anderson."

"I don't know about that. If he was totally smashed, it seems unlikely he would have been able to come up with such a far-fetched story, unless it was true. Anderson also said he clammed up about it afterward, once he sobered up."

Clint's eyes grew troubled and he stared off toward the mountains. "Even if it is true, and she's not his actual legal wife, I'm not sure if it makes much of a difference. What am I supposed to do with that information? If anything."

"We could always go look it up," I suggested. "You said they lived here, in Winterspell, right?"

"Yes. Our family had a summer home here when we were growing up. After our parents divorced, our mother opted to make the lake house her permanent residence. I'd say it was about a year ago that Seth moved here, bought a house, was planning to put down roots." Clint's jaw flexed. I wondered if he was still recalling all of the cruel things his brother's ghost had said back in my kitchen. Days had passed since the seance, but barbed words like that tended to stick around for a while.

"Well, in that case, the marriage should have been filed with the records office here in town," I told him. "Even if it was a destination wedding, like you mentioned, the marriage would have been put into the magical system for record-keeping purposes."

Clint looked suddenly excited. "What time do they close?"

"Six o'clock."

Clint checked his watch. "That's in forty minutes. Do we have enough time to get there?"

I smiled. "That's one perk of living in a small town, most everything is only a few minutes away. Come on."

I drove my car in the lead so Clint could easily follow in his rented sedan. The Chalet was a good twenty minutes from the heart of Winterspell, but we still arrived with plenty of time before the office closed. Clint parked beside me and hurried ahead in order to hold open the door for me. I smiled at him as I passed through into the small, rectangular building. It was the very picture of utilitarian design.

The interior was just as bland as the exterior, save for Petunia, the brightly colored fairy who ran the place. A small desk sat up front, and behind it were rows upon rows of metal filing cabinets that stretched from floor to ceiling. The Order of the Arcane eschewed technology and insisted on everything being written down by hand and physically stored in records offices like this one, all around the world. I guess the sight of how much space that actually took up must have gotten to Clint, because he looked downright flummoxed.

Behind the small desk sat Petunia, her shock of electric purple hair concealing her face as she bent over the desk, scribbling on a tablet of paper. Iridescent green wings flexed and twitched from her back, catching glimmers of the fading sunlight through the office's solitary window.

Petunia glanced up at our entrance, her crystal blue eyes going wide behind her hot pink wire-framed glasses. Petunia was a different type of fairy than Julia the coffee slinger, and was a bit larger. She was roughly the size of a house cat, and about as cute.

"Hey Cora," she said with a sunny smile. Her eyes fell on Clint and her smile grew wider. "Helloooo!"

Instantly she flitted up from behind the desk and came up beside Clint. "I don't believe we've met. I'm Petunia. Has anybody ever told you that you look like Peter Petrelli from *Heroes*?"

"Um, no," Clint said nervously, shrinking back from the eager fairy.

"Because," Petunia said as if Clint hadn't spoken, "I've written sooo much fanfiction about Peter

Petrelli. Granted, a lot of it also featured Sylar, but—"

"Petunia," I said gently.

"Oh! Cora, I didn't mean anything by it—I wasn't trying to hit on your boy—er, *man*friend."

"What? Oh, no. No, it's not like that, it's just—" I paused and slid a glance toward Clint, hoping he would jump in and bail me out.

He smiled and extended a hand toward the fairy. "I'm Clint Bridges. Cora is helping me with something, and she thought you might be able to assist us both."

"Clint Bridges?" Petunia repeated, as though she couldn't quite place it.

I stumbled ahead, hoping she wouldn't have time to connect the dots and bring up the feature the *Winterspell Gazette* had run last week on the murder investigation. "Uh, listen, Petunia, I was hoping you could check and see if there was a particular marriage certificate on file."

"Of course!" Petunia's wings fluttered with delight. "I would be happy to help. Whose marriage certificate are you looking for?"

"My brother. Seth Bridges."

"I swear I've heard that name recently." She frowned, but didn't dwell on it too long before she popped up from the desk and buzzed across the room to access one of the metal cabinets. "Let's see here ... Baskin, Becker, Butler ..."

She checked through the names once more, slower on the second pass, before she looked up from the cabinet. "Sorry. I don't seem to have a marriage certificate listed under that name on file."

Clint gave me a look. I pursed my lips in thought. "Wait a minute. Maybe we can come at this from a different angle. Your brother and his wife owned their house, right?"

"Right."

"Then the deed should be on file here. Can you check that same last name, but in the property records section?" I asked.

Petunia shook her head and pixie dust fell to the floor. "I'd need the address. Do you know it?"

Clint pulled a cell phone from the interior pocket of his jacket.

"You got your phone back?" I asked.

"Day before yesterday," he replied, not looking up from the screen as he flipped through his own virtual records. "You can erase the number from my hotel room. I'll give you this one instead." He glanced up, his eyes a little worried. "If you want it, I mean."

I smiled. "Of course, I do. Why wouldn't I?"

"Well, it's just—" He paused and slid a glance at the small fairy who had silently flown so close to us that her nose was nearly pressed up against Clint's shoulder.

She straightened and buzzed back a couple of feet when she saw Clint look at her. "Sorry. Bad habit," she said with a nervous titter of laughter.

"Here's the address," Clint said, turning away from me in order to jot the address down on a piece of stray paper atop Petunia's desk.

With a pair of rosy cheeks, Petunia flew off to work. It didn't take her long to come up with the deed to Seth's house.

"Take a look at this," I said, tapping the paper. "They aren't listed as married, and Melissa has a different last name."

"Well, maybe they bought the house before they got married?" Clint frowned thoughtfully. "I wasn't all that involved in my brother's life in recent years."

"Couldn't you ask your mother?" I asked.

"I could if she were speaking to me. Which she isn't." Clint sighed. "It's like being a pariah in my own home."

Petunia was buzzing awfully close again, so I thanked her for the help, and got Clint out of there before she figured out what we were talking about.

Once outside in the minuscule parking lot, Clint dragged both hands through his hair. "Seth, what were you up to?" he muttered, seemingly to himself.

"We could try conjuring him back up to ask," I suggested. "Last time we were asking him to give us information he legitimately didn't know. Surely he can tell us whether or not he was actually married to Melissa?"

Clint's eyes grew distant as he considered my offer. At length he nodded. "All right. I guess it couldn't hurt to try. Though I don't know why he'd tell me the truth when he's been lying to everyone else. I mean, he made it pretty plain how he felt about me. I'm not exactly one of his confidants."

"I know," I said gently, "but he also has no motivation to lie to you about this, and who knows, maybe he's starting to get his memories back. I'm honestly not sure how any of this Shadow Realm stuff works. I tried to ask Selene more about it, but … well, you know how she is by now."

A hint of a smile tugged at Clint's lips. "She's a little prickly, isn't she?"

I laughed. "That's the understatement of the year."

His smile widened and I felt a bit of relief. He was carrying around some seriously heavy burdens.

It was nice to know I could make him forget about the weight, even just for a moment or two.

Clint glanced up the street. "Uh, do you think we could do it at your place? My hotel room's a little cramped."

"Of course."

We drove back to my place in our respective vehicles. Selene was not-so-patiently waiting for me on the porch, her eyes glowing in the ever-dimming evening light. "Well, it's about time. I was about to send out a search party for you," she scolded as I got out of my car and closed the door.

"I told you where I was going," I replied. "I even offered to let you tag along. You said you would rather wait at home."

"Yeah, because that hoity-toity hotel won't let me inside, and I'm not about to be left to broil in that trash receptacle on wheels," she fired back, giving my car a pointed look.

I rolled my eyes. "It was *one* time, Selene, and we both know I cleaned up right after it happened."

Clint chuckled as he came to join us. "Should I ask?"

I exhaled. "About a week after Selene came to live with me, we were going to my mom's house in the car. I'd been pulling really late nights at the shop, and basically living on takeout, so yes, I'll admit, there were a few boxes and bags crumpled up in the backseat. Anyway, we were driving to my mom's for dinner and Selene accidentally stepped on a ketchup packet. Her claw punctured it and she got a *drop* of it in her fur, and ever since, she talks about my car as if it were some trash heap."

"It was more than a drop and you know it, Cora." Selene shuddered at the memory.

I shook my head, then unlocked the front door. "In any case, you survived. Lucky me."

Clint chuckled and followed me inside.

"What's going on here, anyway?" Selene asked, trotting ahead of both of us. "Don't tell me this is some kind of date. I refuse to be the third wheel."

Clint smiled at me and a pair of butterflies scooped through my stomach. "Unfortunately, no. We were hoping you might help us conjure a ghost again."

Selene eyed him. "What's in it for me this time?"

"Oh." Clint blinked. He clearly hadn't considered she would want something else out of him. Nothing was ever free with Selene.

"We don't need her help this time," I said. "I remember the spells."

Selene's mouth dropped open but she couldn't seem to form any words.

I chuckled. "What? You got your own tongue?"

"You—I mean, I never—to think—" Selene sputtered. She paused and shook her head. "The audacity, to think you are some kind of master, after a single successful effort at reaching the Shadow Realm. Humph! This must be that gold-star generation thing people are always complaining about."

"If you don't think I'm capable, you are more than free to supervise," I said, giving Clint a wink when Selene wasn't looking my way.

He smiled, clued in to the game.

In truth, while I remembered the gist of the spell, I wouldn't dare try it without Selene's guidance. There was no telling what kind of mess we might find ourselves in if it went wrong. But at the same time, doing it this way, she couldn't take advantage of Clint and make a money grab.

"I should think so," she huffed, already off to the kitchen to begin the preparations.

"FEELS like we're old hats at this now," Clint said once we had everything gathered, just like before. He held a clean paper towel to his pricked finger, while we waited for the tea to steep.

I smiled. "Yeah, I know what you mean. Maybe we can start a side business. Tea with your ancestors."

"I guarantee there's not a domain name out there called 'teawithyourancestors.com,' either," Clint replied.

We chuckled and made small talk until Selene snapped at us to get back on task. Soon the watery outline of mist appeared again, gradually coalescing into the vaguely translucent form of Seth Bridges.

"Did you call me back just so you can 'hang up' on me again?" He harrumphed with great indignity, clearly feeling put upon.

"Sorry about that," I said quickly. "We need your help, Seth. I'm sorry to disturb you, but—"

"Are you kidding? Do you know how boring the afterlife is? Everyone around me seems to have gone mute. Even Granddad is freezing me out. He won't let me join his poker ring either, old fool."

"Don't make me spill your tea already, Seth," Selene warned.

"Listen, Seth," Clint said. "I really need to talk to you."

Seth groaned. "I told you, I don't know who killed me! Maybe it was the head injury, I don't know, but I can't help you."

"That's not what I needed to talk to you about." Clint swallowed hard. "Seth, were you really married to Melissa?"

Seth flinched. "Of course I was! You saw the photos. We eloped down in Cabo."

"I saw the photos, all right, but what I didn't see was a marriage certificate on file down at the record's office. Would you care to explain that?"

Seth's eyes narrowed to slits. "Well, maybe that's because we got married in Mexico, not here. Did you ever think of that, Mr. Smart Guy?"

Clint sighed. "Look, Seth, you might as well come clean. Anderson sold you out. He told us all about your sham marriage."

Seth deflated. He even seemed to grow more translucent, like he weakened ectoplasmically along with every other way.

"I—" he sighed. "Okay. It's all true. I only pretended to get married to Melissa."

"Why?" I shook my head. "Why go through with the sham?"

"I was under immense pressure to get married. Mom just wouldn't stop hounding me about it. For a long time, I thought she was just eager for grand-kids, you know? Then, I found out the truth."

"What truth?" I prompted when he lapsed into silence.

"Mom's health wasn't getting any better. I think she liked the idea of seeing grandkids before she died, or maybe just seeing me getting married would have been enough."

"Why Melissa?"

Seth cast his eyes downward. "We met a few years ago, at work. I wanted her. Badly. But she put me in the friend zone. When I realized that the way to get what I wanted from Mother was through a diamond ring, well, I made Melissa an offer to split the inheritance money. I thought … I thought that if she 'pretend married' me, she'd eventually grow to truly love me, the way that I loved her."

"Whew. This guy's a few biscuits short of a picnic," Selene quipped.

Seth shook his incorporeal head. "It was work-ing, too. Mother adores Melissa, just like I knew she would. I think Melissa cares for her as well."

"But your relationship never changed?" I asked.

Seth looked away, his jaw tensed. "No. We had a

couple of drunken nights where I would wake up the next morning, thinking I'd finally won her over, only for her to say it was all a mistake and push me away again."

"Is that why you had an affair?" I asked softly. "With the redheaded bartender?"

"Penny." Seth's face contorted in misery. "She was a good time. Nothing more. All I wanted was to make Melissa jealous. I thought maybe if she thought she was losing me, she'd realize she cared. That's why I never bothered trying to hide the affair. I *wanted* Melissa to find out about it."

Selene scoffed. "Is there such a thing as an anti-self-help book? Because, if so, this guy really missed his calling."

"Selene," I scolded.

Sure, Seth was still a bottom feeder in my estimation, purely for the way he'd spoken to Clint, but he was pouring out his real emotions. Mocking him for his foolishness seemed a little too mean.

Seth covered his face with his hand. Given the fact that he was translucent, the effect was somewhat diminished. "My word ... I've spent my whole life living a lie, and I even dragged my mother and Penny into it. There's no doubt I'm reaping what I've sown. I'm sorry I got mad and accused you of killing me, Clint."

Suddenly, Seth was bathed in a golden light so bright I could barely stand to look at him. His face stretched into a smile as he stared directly into the blinding light. "It's so beautiful! So beautiful ..."

Then he was gone. Selene groaned in annoyance.

"Great. What a time for that miscreant to reach enlightenment. He's gone to the Stardust Realm. Out of our reach. Forever."

"At least he confirmed Anderson's story," I said.

"Yeah, at least." Clint sighed.

16

*M*y living room quickly took on the appearance of a war room. Files, facts, and figures lay scrawled on bits of sticky notes adhered to every available surface. I had practically wallpapered one side of the room with them. Now and again a breeze would blow through the picture window and knock a few to the floor.

"Ugh," I scoffed, picking up the latest runaway. "I'd close the window, but it's still pretty warm in here and I don't have AC."

"It's fine. Although, it is starting to get a little bit of a *Homeland* season one vibe in here," Clint teased as he came into the living room with two glasses of iced tea. "Are you all right?"

I held up a finger to forestall further questions. "I'm fine. Just … give me a second to set this all up."

Clint nodded and set the glasses onto two coasters on the coffee table before he sat down on the couch. Selene was oddly subdued, watching me move around the den like a ping pong ball on steroids. At last, I stood back and surveyed my handiwork. I'd created a timeline of the events surrounding Seth's murder, along with important clues and suspects.

Okay, maybe Selene was right. I did need to dial back my consumption of TV cop shows.

I'd start tomorrow.

As it was, I felt like we had everything we needed to solve the case and get to the truth. It was just a matter of getting the right perspective, and somehow having it all on paper helped my brain process things a little better.

"Okay." I put my hands on my hips and faced the sofa. "This is all the evidence, notes, and theories I've put together. Let's break them down one by one and see if we can't find our killer."

I turned and gestured at the paper-covered hearth, bereft of a fire in the summer. "Theory number one—"

"I have a question," Selene said sweetly. Too

sweetly. I knew I was going to get messed with, but I went ahead and put that hook right in my mouth anyway.

"Go ahead, Selene."

"Which theory presents the scenario where Clint is the killer?"

I frowned. "None of them, Selene."

"Um, why not?" Selene's tail twitched back and forth like a pendulum. "I mean, let's look at the evidence. His fingerprints are on the murder weapon, he was at the victim's house the night of the murder, and he had motive after being cut out of his mother's will."

I wiped a hand down my face. "Thanks, Selene. I'm sure Clint appreciates that."

Clint winced. "I'll admit, it's going to take some rock-solid proof to even have a shot at getting the detective to focus on someone other than me."

"Unfortunately, you don't have an alibi," I said, "but the fact that you bought the gift basket means your fingerprints are on the murder weapon. For that matter, *I* could be the killer, since my prints were on it, too."

Selene popped up her head. "Luckily, you have me to serve as your alibi. As I recall, you came home after work, scarfed down a sad TV dinner, then an entire sleeve of Oreo cookies, and watched reality shows until you fell asleep—and drooled, might I add—right here on this very couch."

I closed my eyes and silently counted to four to keep myself from hurling her in a wind cyclone right out into the lake. "First of all, it was *not* an entire sleeve of Oreos—"

Selene cocked her head to one side.

"Okay, fine, it was, but in my defense, it was a rough night, okay? And we're getting way off track!" I groaned. "Anyway, as I was saying, the prints alone won't be enough for an arrest warrant, or they would have already taken you into custody."

Clint was smiling as he looked between Selene and me, but he sobered slightly as I steered us back to the matter at hand. "My lawyer says all they need is one more piece of evidence, even circumstantial, to make the arrest. It literally could come any day now."

I swallowed hard. "Right. Well, as far as motive goes, I think we can make an argument that Clint is well off financially enough that that shouldn't be a factor."

"Fair enough," Selene replied. "I'll allow it."

"When did this turn into *Judge Judy*?" I groused.

"Now, see, there's a woman after my own heart,"

Selene purred. "She speaks her mind. She doesn't take anyone's crap."

"Yes, quite an idol." I rolled my eyes, then tapped my wall of sticky notes. "Can we please focus here? My first theory involves Seth's business partner, Anderson."

I gestured to the evidence tree. "Anderson was at Seth's house the night of the murder, giving him opportunity. We also know they argued that night, remember? Seth said he needed a drink alone in his study to relax afterward."

Clint nodded. "That was also the reason why I didn't actually go inside that night when I stopped by. I went there to talk to Seth, but Melissa told me he was in the middle of something. I left without seeing him, but according to the police, some neighbor reported seeing me at the house, which they're using to place me at the scene of the crime."

"Right." I nodded, and gestured to another note that had a line scrawled about the neighbor. "Anderson also scores high on the motive chart," I added. "He wanted to buy Seth out of his share of their business, Seth refused. Now the whole company belongs to Anderson and he doesn't have to fight for it. That's significant."

"I agree with you that on paper it makes sense,

but Anderson didn't seem to be acting guilty," Clint interjected. "He honestly seemed broken up about the situation."

"Pish posh," Selene replied. "That doesn't mean anything."

"Seth said he went to the study to get a drink *after* the argument though," I pointed out. "It didn't sound like Anderson was still in the house at that point. So, unless he left, then came back to kill him, I'm not sure that theory holds too much water. Plus, if he killed him, why bother sticking around for the funeral? Wouldn't he want to get out of Winterspell as quickly as possible?"

"All right, so if it wasn't me, and it wasn't Anderson, who is left?" Clint asked before taking a sip of his iced tea. "Anderson said Seth had alienated his friends."

"I wrote down that it could have been a random intruder, but it doesn't really make a lot of sense. Nothing was stolen from the house, which would rule out robbery as a motive. Plus, in a tight-knit community like this one, where much of the population can use magic, random home invasions are exceedingly rare."

"I think it's clear that the killer had a personal grudge." Selene sounded dead serious for a change.

"Thank you, Selene, that was a useful comment for once—"

"You know who might have something personal against Seth?" Selene asked sweetly. "How about the guy who got cut out of the will?"

I rubbed a hand down my face and sighed. "Selene …"

"It's all right, she doesn't mean anything by it. She's just messing with the new guy. Like hazing." Clint smiled as if it were no big deal, but I was still miffed on his behalf.

"There really is only one person left," I said, a little hesitant to bring it forward. I pointed at a sticky note near the end of my collage. "Melissa."

Clint didn't seem completely surprised, but he also didn't look convinced.

"Now, at first, I skipped over her because of how upset she seemed at book club. But the more I think about it, the more I'm struggling to recall if she shed any *actual* tears, or if it was a lot of sniffling and burying her face in her hands. I mean, honestly, if my husband was murdered, the last place I would go is book club!"

"Ha! You could be on your deathbed and still try to find a way to get ahold of some of Judy's crab cakes," Selene interrupted.

I shot her a dark look, but pressed on. "She's not even a regular at book club. I go every month—"

"For said crab cakes," Selene said with a grin.

"—and I think I've only seen her there a couple of times. I didn't even know her name. And it's not a huge group. What if she was only there to make an appearance, to play the part of the grieving spouse? You heard what Seth said, they weren't really married or in love. So, unless his death hit her a lot harder than Seth would have expected, she was acting. Playing it up for a crowd of sympathetic housewives."

"You may be on to something," Clint said, "but just because she's a drama queen, and possibly milking sympathy from book club, doesn't mean she's a killer."

"Fair enough, so let's look at the motive and opportunity. First, the motive: Why should she be happy with half the inheritance from the sham wedding, when she could have it all?"

Clint shook his head. "That doesn't make any sense, though. Melissa has been really sweet the handful of times I've seen her. She's the one who was trying to get me and Seth to patch things up after our estrangement." He fell silent for a moment, then added, "She called me that night."

My eyes widened. "She did?"

"She felt bad that Seth and I didn't get a chance to talk when I stopped by, because he was busy with Anderson. She said she knew I was staying at a hotel in town, and wondered if I wanted to get together with her to talk about Seth. According to her, she left the house not long after turning me away, and went out to run some errands. She said she didn't want to go back home and listen to Seth and Anderson argue. At first, I turned her down and told her I was busy with some work stuff in my hotel room—which was true. But she convinced me to meet her anyway."

Clint paused and exhaled. "Anyway, she said she had to drop the groceries off at home, and that she would meet me at the lake so we could walk and talk. I fired off a few emails, then left my hotel room and went to the lake, by the bench she told me about, near one of the foot trails. I waited for probably half an hour, by myself. To be frank, I was getting a little annoyed with how long it was taking her. I'd left my work in a bit of a fragile spot to meet with her, and it seemed like she was blowing me off."

"So, what happened? Did she ever show up?"

Clint shook his head. "No. The next thing I knew,

my mother was calling me, in absolute hysterics, saying her baby boy was gone."

"Oh." I swallowed.

"In hindsight, I assumed Melissa went home to drop off her groceries, and that was when she found Seth dead. Which explained why she didn't show up to meet me."

"Did you tell the police any of this?" I asked.

He nodded. "Of course, but at that park bench, it wasn't like there were any witnesses to back up my account. They said the phone records only proved that I knew Seth was alone, and that there was an opportunity for me to strike." Clint bit off the end of the sentence with a disgusted huff.

"Sounds like she set you up good," Selene commented, licking one of her front paws. "Trussed you up like a juicy Christmas goose."

I hated when Selene was right, but she was making a lot of sense. "She lured you out of your hotel room, possibly in hopes of other guests seeing you leave, right around the time of the murder. Then she had you go to a remote location with no witnesses to corroborate that you weren't at your brother's house on the other side of town. Although, what about the cell towers? Could that prove you weren't at the house?"

"I don't think so, but I can ask my lawyer about it," Clint replied, looking more miserable than I'd ever seen him before.

"So we have motive, what about opportunity? She's the one who discovered the body, so she obviously had the opportunity to do the murder herself," I said, considering my notes once more.

"Melissa isn't a large woman," Clint interjected. "How could she have overpowered my brother? He had to be at least five or six inches taller than her, and have a good fifty pounds on her, too."

I considered it for a moment, then was hit with a sick realization. "The tranquility candle."

Clint canted his head. "What?"

"The candle. It was one of the ones you bought for your mother. The one that creates the illusion of a meadow at night. It uses one of the deepest relaxation spells I know. The officer who came to my shop showed me a photo of one burned down to the wick on Seth's desk. So, let's say he went into his study, drink in hand, and lit the candle—he wouldn't be unconscious or totally unaware, of course, but he trusted Melissa. He wouldn't have thought anything of her walking up behind him—"

I shut my mouth, refusing to continue with the gruesome tale.

"That's … disturbing," Clint said. "I can't believe she would do something so ruthless."

"Money makes people do terrible things, sometimes," I said softly.

"Don't you think the police looked into her?" Selene asked Clint. "Isn't that always the first suspect? The spouse or partner?"

"I think they did," Clint replied. "I heard through the grapevine that she had some receipts from the market and the gas station that supposedly gave her an alibi."

Selene scoffed. "She's the one who found the body. She could have killed him, run out to fabricate the alibi, and returned home just in time to kick off the first act of her new starring role as the pitiful, grieving widow."

Clint looked to me. I cringed and offered a half-hearted shrug. "It's not a pretty picture, but it's the only theory that makes much sense right now."

"The problem is, we don't have a way to be sure it was her."

I nodded. "There must be a way to get her to confess."

"What about your True Desire candles?" Clint asked.

"They're not lie detectors, remember?" Selene sneered.

"No, no, I was about to suggest the same thing." I tapped a finger along my lips. "Under the right circumstances, the True Desire candle might be enough to at least get the investigators to take a second look. We just have to arrange those right circumstances."

"Yes, but how?" Clint spread his hands out wide. "How are we going to do that?"

I pursed my lips in thought. "Clint, you need to call your mother."

"What? I can't do that. She refuses to see me."

"You're going to have to convince her otherwise," I said. "I know it's not pleasant, but you have to."

"Why?" Clint frowned in dismay. It was clear he did not relish the idea.

"Because, if we're going to prove your innocence, and Melissa's guilt, we're going to need your mother's help."

17

I watched Clint call his mother, and got a solid dose of secondhand anxiety. His tension was palpable and bled over into me as well.

Selene of course offered no sympathy. "What's so hard about saying, 'Hi Mom, I know you think I'm guilty of fratricide but guess what, I'm not, and I need your help to prove it'?"

Clint pursed his lips in a frown at the cat. The volume on his phone was high enough I could hear his mother answer the other end.

"Why do you keep calling me? I told you to leave me alone."

"Wait, please, Mother, don't hang up. Listen to me for a minute."

"All right," she snapped. "What is so important?"

Clint's face turned red. He stammered, stumbled over several attempts to speak. Finally he looked at Selene as if in a flash of sudden inspiration.

"Listen, I know you think I'm guilty of killing Seth, but I'm not, and I need your help to prove it."

A long silence stretched out while I hid my face in my hand. Of all the times for someone to take Selene's smarminess seriously ...

"What exactly do you expect me to do?" The voice on the other line sounded borderline hostile, but at least she was still talking and hadn't ended the call. Under the circumstances, I took this as a good sign.

"It would be a lot easier to explain it to you in person," Clint said. "Can I come over?"

Another long silence. "I don't know if that's appropriate."

"I don't know what you've been told, but I'm your son. Shouldn't my word count for anything?"

There was a prolonged silence before the woman's sharp voice replied, "You say you can prove it?"

"Yes. I swear—" Clint's voice broke and his eyes grew glassy. "Please, just give me a chance."

"All right," his mother said with a resigned sigh.

"Thank you." He glanced at me. "Um, I'm bringing company, is that okay?"

"I hope it's your lawyer," his mother said, and then hung up.

Clint turned to me with a haunted expression in his eyes. "I really hope you know what you're doing, Cora."

Yeah, that makes two of us, I thought to myself, but kept it from reaching my lips. Clint was stressed enough, he needed me to be the steady rock for the time being.

We piled into my car and drove to the candle shop. I ducked inside long enough to grab my True Desire candle, the one with the longest wick in my shop. Once I had the necessary candle, I climbed back behind the wheel and we headed for Clint's mother's lake house. During the drive, Clint became increasingly nervous. He drummed fingers on the dashboard, stared out the window, and fidgeted in his seat. I could feel the nervous energy coming off of him in waves.

"It's going to be okay," I told him at one point.

He offered a tight-lipped smile in response, but then went back to tapping his fingers on his thigh.

The only hiccup was that the entirety of our plan rested on Clint's mother's shoulders. If she turned us away once we explained what we'd found out, the rest of it would fall apart.

Which also made me wonder why his mother was so dead set on him being the guilty party. Was there something in Clint that I wasn't seeing? Did he have a torrid history of violence that he now kept concealed by expensive suits and a charming smile? It was unnerving to think I might be missing something.

At the same time, I didn't want to pepper him with questions about his relationship with his mother. He'd already explained that he was estranged, both from her and his brother. He'd blamed it on his work, but there had to be more to the story. I would have to be patient and draw it out slowly. At present, I didn't want him to think I was turning on him. The truth was, I believed him. My gut told me he wasn't a killer, and my gut was usually a very good judge of character.

We pulled up outside the lake house just after sundown. The house was impressive and made me even more curious just how much money was on the line. The manor sat on a spacious, gated lot. The lake was just on the other side of this grove of estates, meaning that nearly every window in the house would have a water view. I also imagined a sprawling backyard with Adirondack chairs gathered around a fire pit, a large deck for entertaining, and perhaps even a private dock.

It was the stuff dreams were made of. Although, I noted with a macabre addendum, in this case, it could very well be the impetus for this terrible nightmare. Money could buy a lot of things, but it couldn't guarantee a happy family or secure eternal loyalty and love.

As we exited the car, I noticed a large robin perched near a pinecone off to one side of the wide driveway, its black eyes seeming to judge us as we walked up to the front door.

"Well, here goes nothing," Clint said as he lifted the brass loop mounted to the door. His face twisted into a wry, mirthless grin. "I've never had to knock before. I've always just walked in."

"So, just walk in," Selene suggested.

"Doesn't feel like I have the right to, at the moment. At least not as far as my mother is concerned."

My heart swelled with pity for the man. I reached out and patted his arm. "Let's see if we can't get you back that right."

He rapped the metal knocker against the wood a few times, then we stood back and waited. It seemed as if the ten seconds or so that it took for Clint's mother to answer the door lasted for an agonizing eternity. Particularly for Clint.

The door swung open and a well-preserved looking woman confronted us. Normally, I wasn't one to judge plastic surgery. I figured it was none of my business what anyone did to their own body. But by my estimate, Mrs. Bridges had crossed over the line into *too much* a few procedures ago. Her skin was so tight across her bony face it looked physically painful.

Through it all, I could still tell that she and Clint had the same eyes, though hers were filled with barely pent-up anger. "Clint."

She flicked her cold gaze over to me. "I recognize you. You're the candle lady."

"I guess that makes me the candle lady's cat," Selene said, pushing her way inside. "You going to stand there with the door open all day, letting the flies in?"

Clint's mother did a double take at the pushy cat now making her way across the marble foyer. I resisted the urge to rubberneck around their well-appointed home. Let's just say that their wealth was obvious, if not overt. They had a lot of the same things I had in my own house, just fancier.

She led us into her living room, and I was surprised to discover there was tea. Clint's mother made a point of pouring herself and me a cup of tea, but eschewed doing so for her own son. He eventually sighed and leaned forward toward the coffee table to make his own cup.

"Now, what is it you have to tell me?" she asked bluntly. Her eyes were full of accusation, as if to say she seriously doubted we could tell her anything, anything at all that might change her mind.

Clint struggled to speak, afraid to even look his mother in the eye. I could relate, as she seemed a fearsome woman. However, all his behavior did was make him look even more guilty in her eyes.

"Clint," I prompted. "Show your mother the deed to Seth's house."

"The deed?" Clint's mother's eyes narrowed to slits. "Is this about the will? You think after what happened, I'm going to cut you back in—"

"That's not what this is about," Clint said swiftly. "I mean, I've already said I don't care about the money. I have plenty on my own."

"For now," she muttered. "Seth tells me—" The woman paused, a flicker of emotion somehow managing to break through all the fillers and Botox.

"Seth *told* me you were struggling to bring on new clients."

"Seth and I never talked business," Clint said, his voice nearly a growl. "How would he even know?"

I cleared my throat. "Mrs. Bridges, will you please—"

"It's Ms. Cleaver," the woman interrupted tartly.

"How appropriate," Selene muttered from her place on the floor.

"Ms. Cleaver," I hurried to say, "Will you please look at the deed? Specifically the signature line?"

She sighed and reached into her pocket for a pair of reading glasses. "All right, I'll play along, but I don't see where this is going."

She scrutinized the deed for a long moment, then looked up in disgust. "It has the names of my dead son and his widow on it. So what?"

"Yes, but look at the last name on Melissa's signature and printed verification."

Clint's mother made a big show of sighing and taking another look through her reading glasses. Her eyes squinted behind the red-rimmed lenses. Again she scoffed and yanked the glasses off her face. "So she used her maiden name when she signed. Is this supposed to be some sort of smoking gun? What could this possibly have to do with my son's murder?"

"Everything," I said. She snapped her hawkish gaze my way and I swallowed hard. "I know this is going to sound strange, and might be hard to believe, but—"

"Oh for goodness' sake, will you just spit it out?" she snarled.

I swallowed again, trying not to let my voice break when I spoke. "Seth and Melissa's marriage wasn't real."

Her face contorted in a suspicious grimace. "I don't follow you. What do you mean, it wasn't real?"

She pointed her finger at the front door. "Should I bring Melissa over here so she can break down in miserable sobbing because her husband is dead? Their marriage seemed pretty real to me."

Clint cleared his throat. "When we went to the records office, we asked for a copy of Seth and Melissa's marriage certificate. It's not on file."

Ms. Cleaver waved a dismissive hand. "So, they forgot to file some paperwork. They're hardly the first magical couple to wed in the non-magic world and forget to notify the Order."

"The wedding photos were staged!" Clint burst out.

His mother's eyes went wide. "That's quite an accusation, young man."

He ran a hand over his face. "Mother, listen, his business partner told us that Seth confessed the whole thing to him after a night of drinking. The paperwork—or, rather lack thereof—only confirms Anderson's account. The marriage was a ploy to try and get you to change your will. You've never made it a secret that you wanted Seth and me to settle down, have children. Live the way you wanted us to. Seth thought that by fitting into that mold, you would show him favor."

"So, what? Melissa was only *pretending* to be his wife?" Ms. Cleaver shook her head.

"Yes, that's exactly what she's been doing, and we have reason to believe she might know more than she's letting on about his death," Clint added.

His mother's face fell slack. "I—I don't believe it. Why would he tell such an outrageous lie, just for money? Are you saying I didn't know my son at all?"

"He had all of us fooled," Clint said gently. "I never would have suspected he would go to such lengths, but you have to admit, it worked. As soon as he got married and Melissa announced she was expecting their first child, you called me here to change your will, and—"

"I'm dying, Clint."

The words seemed to reverberate somehow, as if they had a physical weight to them that slammed into the room like a sledgehammer.

Clint's mouth hung open. "I—I don't understand."

Ms. Cleaver's face became a grim mask of anger and grief. "I called you here in hopes of sitting you and your brother down and telling you the truth. Yes, I made changes to the will, to grant your brother more because I knew I most likely would not be around to dote on my first grandchild. I wanted to make sure they had everything they needed to raise their baby properly."

Selene slinked out of the room, and I desperately wished I could follow. This wasn't a conversation meant for me to observe. But I feared that getting up and leaving would somehow make it more awkward and painful. There was also a part of me that didn't want to leave Clint alone in the aftermath of his mother's news.

"It's cancer," Ms. Cleaver continued, her eyes glassy.

"I'm so sorry, Mother," Clint finally said. He started to reach for her hand, but then pulled away. "I had no idea."

"Well, you wouldn't, would you?" she replied, her

voice turning sharp again. "You're never here. You don't call. Write. I have no idea what's going on in your life, besides the fact that you live in a fancy condominium and go to work in an office."

Clint looked down at the floor between them for a prolonged moment. When he looked up again, a single tear had worked its way down his cheek. "Is there anything I can do?"

"No." Ms. Cleaver shook her head with an air of defiance. "I'm perfectly capable of taking care of myself. I've arranged for a live-in nurse to come when the worst of it arrives. And, of course, Melissa has offered to help in any way she can."

Clint's jaw tensed. "I know you don't want to hear this, and the last thing I want to do is cause you more pain, but Mother, please, you have to believe me. Melissa is not who she says she is."

Ms. Cleaver's cold stare slid back into place and she shot it at Clint with a renewed fervor. "How dare you?" She sputtered. "Melissa is like my own daughter. I love her just as much as I loved my son!"

Clint looked resigned. On a heavy exhale, he got to his feet. "I'm truly sorry for all of this, but I'm not going to drop this until Melissa answers some questions. I won't take the fall for something I didn't do, and I did not kill Seth."

"And you think Melissa did, is that it?"

"It looks like it. Yes."

I shifted nervously. "Clint and I think we have found a way to get her to confess …"

I looked to Clint. "But we need your help."

"I'm not going to act against my daughter-in-law," she said firmly.

"You don't have to, "I said quickly. "All you have to do is invite her over, watch, and listen."

Clint's voice wavered as he spoke his final plea, "Give us this chance, and if we can't convince you, I promise to leave and never darken your door again, if that's what you want."

Ms. Cleaver gave us a long, lingering look, her expression inscrutable. Then, barely perceptibly, she nodded her assent.

18

I paced across the living room, nervously fidgeting with my hands while awaiting Melissa's arrival. Clint sat on the sofa, somewhat dazed. I couldn't read the look in his eyes, but even I was reeling after his mother's news, and I was a virtual stranger. For her part, his mother sat in a chair, her spine ramrod straight as she elegantly sipped at her tea, occasionally glancing out into the foyer.

"Are you sure she's coming?" Clint asked his mother.

"She said she was," his mother replied. "I don't know what else to tell you. She told me she was coming, and I have no reason to believe she won't be here soon."

Clint fell silent once more. His mother gave him the side-eye while she sipped her tea.

For once, I found myself missing Selene. Sure, she'd likely say something wildly inappropriate, but at least it would crack through the layer of ice that engulfed us.

I suppose I should have been more worried about what the feline in question *was* doing. She'd wandered out in the middle of the family squabble, and hadn't yet circled back around to rejoin us. If Ms. Cleaver thought it odd to have a strange cat wandering her house unassisted, she didn't speak up. Then again, she might have forgotten about Selene entirely.

"What I don't understand is what any of this has to do with you," Ms. Cleaver said, leveling me with a frosty glare as she leaned forward to place her delicate teacup on the table.

I wasn't quite sure how to answer. Had my involvement begun that night at my candle shop, when Clint was shopping and asked me on a date? Or had it been the evening he'd appeared in the alleyway asking to use my computer? Or maybe it was when the officer asked me about the candelabra and the tranquility candles.

"She's a friend," Clint said.

Ms. Cleaver looked at her son, but her stony mask remained in place. "A friend? Someone you knew from our summers here? Because prior to a week ago, you hadn't been to Winterspell in over a decade."

"A *new* friend," Clint clarified. "I met her my first night back in town, when I stopped to get your gift." He paused, a new emotion showing on his face. He canted his head and pinned his mother with a puzzled look. "Which reminds me, what was the candelabra and candle set doing at Seth and Melissa's house in the first place?"

Ms. Cleaver scowled. "I don't care for overly fragrant things in my house, and I thought the candelabra was tacky. Melissa seemed to admire them both, so I told her to take the basket home when they left."

Clint nodded, his jaw tight. "I see."

I glanced over at Clint. "She would have known your prints were on the candelabra. It might explain why she chose it as the murder weapon."

Ms. Cleaver bristled. "We don't know that, yet. Honestly, I'm not sure why I even let you two talk me into going along with this plan."

Outside, a car door slammed.

Clint jumped to his feet. Ms. Cleaver took her

time getting up from her own chair, and went to answer the door before Melissa even had a chance to knock.

"Come in, dear," she greeted the young woman, and they embraced.

Melissa came inside, her several-months'-pregnant belly leading the way. She was all smiles until she stepped far enough inside the house to see through to the living room. As soon as she saw Clint and me, her smile faltered. "Oh," she said, "I didn't know you had company." She narrowed her gaze in my direction. "I know you, don't I? From book club?"

"Cora Hearth," I said.

"Right. Cora." Melissa looked at her brother-in-law. "Clint, I didn't expect you, either. Aren't you—"

"I'm visiting my mother," Clint said firmly.

Melissa inclined her head. "Of course." She looked over her shoulder at Ms. Cleaver.

"It's all right, Melissa," Ms. Cleaver said. "He's not here to cause trouble."

"I don't know that I feel comfortable staying so long as he's here," Melissa replied, her hands going to cradle her belly, as though her unborn child were in danger by Clint's presence.

I turned away and rolled my eyes.

The Heart's Desire candle was still nestled in my purse. I grabbed it and set it on the coffee table, beside the tea service, and casually went about lighting the wick.

"What—what's that?" Melissa asked.

"Oh, I was just showing your mother-in-law a little demonstration of what my candles can do," I replied as innocently as the day I was born.

Melissa put her hands on her hips. "I thought you didn't like fragrances in the house?" she asked her faux mother-in-law.

Ms. Cleaver sighed and went back to her chair. She was tolerating the scene, but made it clear she did not want to be an active participant.

"Ugh, finally," Selene's voice said, followed by the cat herself, strolling back into the room as though she'd been waiting a hundred years.

"What the—" Melissa recoiled.

"Selene, what do you want?" I asked.

"Well, I'd really like to go home and sit on your lap," Selene said. Her eyes went wide. I nodded to myself, stifling a grin. The candle was working.

"So, Melissa," I said, garnering her attention "I was just wondering if you could clear a few things up for me."

Her brow scrunched up in suspicion. "What kind of things?"

"Well, uh … not to be indelicate, but now that Seth has passed on, is there anything you want?"

Melissa's brow creased, as though she thought the question odd, but the magic took over and it smoothed again. Though something changed in her eyes, and when she spoke, her words came out harsh. "All I want is for the old lady to drop dead and leave me a pile of money."

Her hand flew to her mouth.

A sudden crash caused me to turn toward Ms. Cleaver. She'd dropped her teacup, and it shattered on the floor. "Melissa? How—how could you say such a thing?"

It hit Melissa right then and there that she'd been had. For a long moment, she stood there, unsure of what to do with herself.

"We know everything, Melissa," I said. "We know about the fake marriage, about your trying to use receipts as your alibi and trying to make Clint look guilty, the way you manipulated Clint's mother, everything."

Melissa was a pretty woman, but the way her face contorted with hatred sapped away her beauty in an instant as she sneered at me. "You don't know anything!"

"Seth really loved you, Melissa," I said with a sigh. "He was hoping he could change your mind about him and the marriage, that maybe you could be a real family, especially with the baby on the way."

"You think I care?" Melissa scowled. "He was so annoying, always following me around and fawning over my every word. I can't believe I put up with it for as long as I did. But I was willing to hang in there for the money, but when he threatened to cut me out —well, that's when I knew he had to go. I hadn't gone this far to walk away empty-handed."

"He was going to cut you out? He told you that?"

"He'd been drinking. He never could hold his liquor." She scoffed impatiently. "He tried to kiss me. He started saying we could make a real baby together. I'll admit, in the past, we'd fooled around a little when we'd both been drinking, but I was done with that game. And I'd told him that—multiple times. He didn't like that I told him *no*. He raised his voice, told me I was ungrateful and spoiled. That he'd given me everything, and that I should be more appreciative. I got my keys and was going to go for a drive, but right before I left the house, he told me that if I walked out the door, the money was as good as gone. He'd tell his mother I cheated on him and have me removed from the will."

"So, you decided to kill him?"

Melissa glared at me for a moment, and I worried she was about to stop short, but her anger bubbled over and she barreled ahead. "I wanted him out of my life. *And* I wanted my money."

I pursed my lips. "How did it happen, Melissa?"

Her eyes narrowed to slits. "Anderson flew into town. Seth had been ignoring his calls, so I guess he thought he would show up and leave him no choice but to deal with it. The two of them were arguing, that much was true. When Anderson went to leave the house, he said something to me in passing. He knew about the fake marriage. Seth wasn't supposed to have told anyone. I figured it was only a matter of time before he blabbed to the wrong person—like his brother." Melissa cut a dark look at Clint. "He had to go. I couldn't risk the truth getting out."

Her lips twisted into a sneer. "I wasn't originally planning to pin it on you. That just sort of worked itself out, as if it were meant to be. I still had to be careful, of course, but your mother had sent me home with that gift basket of candles and I saw that heavy candlestick. I knew it was my perfect out. I wore a glove when I did it so the only prints on the candlestick would be yours. I almost lost my nerve, after that first blow, but—"

For a moment, her enraged exterior cracked, revealing a glimmer of horror in her eyes. I guess the memory of beating a man to death kind of sticks with you. She shook her head as if to clear it.

"Then I threw the candlestick away in the trash, knowing the police would find it and lead them straight to Clint's doorstep."

"Wow, you're just confessing everything in front of witnesses," Selene said. "You must be a special kind of stupid."

"No one is going to believe any of you," Melissa sneered. "Clint is wanted for Seth's murder. They have him dead to rights. I honestly have no idea why it's taking them this long to put you in a cage. And as for you—" she flicked a glance at Ms. Cleaver, "—well, if you were to slip and fall down the stairs on your way to go and tell the police, I'd still get my money."

Ms. Cleaver was still in shock, but something about Melissa's statement roused her. "Try again, dear."

Melissa blinked.

"You never married my son. You are not family to

me," Ms. Cleaver said, her voice growing stronger with fresh outrage.

"My name is still in your will," Melissa said with a smirk.

"No, actually, it's not. Melissa *Bridges* is in my will. And seeing as how she seems to be a creation of my imagination, the money will revert to Clint and the various charity organizations I support."

Melissa's eyes flashed with hot anger as she glared at Clint. "It's an oversight. Your lawyer knows who I am—"

"Well, unless you're planning on throwing all of us down the stairs, I think someone will be able to point him toward the official records office. When you can't produce proof of your marriage, in either this world or the human one, I doubt you'll have many options left," Clint said.

"In that case ..."

Melissa clapped her hands, and a flare went off brighter than the sun. I cursed, throwing an arm up to protect my vision though I knew it was too late.

"Big rookie mistake," Selene howled. "Blinding Flash is like the most basic spell in the book, and you fell for it."

"Shut up!" I blinked rapidly, trying to clear the

spots away from my vision. "Do something useful and watch my back."

I howled as something hard thudded me in the chest. I was thrown to the floor as another thud connected, and I realized they weren't objects, but powerful blows of magic force.

"You just got hit two times," Selene offered helpfully.

Suddenly, a wall of flames burst to life, blocking the living room from the rest of the house. Panic spiked in my chest. I was an air witch. I couldn't fight against fire. Anything I did would only make it worse.

Ms. Cleaver screamed and scurried for the opposite archway, only for a new wall of flames to erupt.

"This way!" Clint yelled from the other side of the room. He threw open a window and began kicking at the screen.

Selene raced ahead toward the window, stopping only to look back over her shoulder to make sure I was coming. I was about to urge her on ahead when her eyes went huge and a *crack* of magic exploded through the room. The blast sent me sideways a good four feet, a split second before one of the wooden beams stretching across the ten-foot ceiling burst into flames.

Selene had saved me from being directly underneath it when the fire ignited.

"Well, don't just sit there staring!" she snapped. "Come on!"

Melissa was nowhere to be seen, but her fire magic was running wild, clearly intent on swallowing all four of us whole. Selene slipped out the window first. Clint looked at me and a silent moment of communication passed between us before he jumped out. His hands stretched back up, "Mother, come on, take my hand. It's not too far."

Ms. Cleaver bridled. "I—I can't—"

We were technically on the first level of the house, but there seemed to be a daylight basement, because the window was a good six feet off the ground.

"Come on, Ms. Cleaver," I sputtered, my eyes watering against the smoke. "We don't have time. I'll help you."

The elderly woman gave me a panicked look and I offered her my hand. She took it and allowed me to help her out the window. I used a bit of air magic at the end, ensuring she landed gently into her son's waiting arms, then I scrambled out after her.

No sooner had my feet hit the ground than a

hand grabbed mine and tugged me across the manicured grass.

"Where is she?" I said, coughing as I looked around.

A car was backing out of the driveway, and a panicked Melissa sat behind the wheel. She hadn't expected us to get free.

Clint bolted toward her.

"Call the police," I shouted to Clint's mother before charging after him.

Melissa exited the car and shot a cannonball of fire at Clint. He dodged at the last moment and it blasted into a boxwood bush planted under one of the windows. She snarled and reloaded her spell.

"What are you doing?" Selene asked, bounding up beside me. "Fight back already!"

"I can't!" I dove for the cover of a stone sculpture as Melissa went after her brother-in-law again. "She's pregnant. Her unborn child hasn't done anything wrong."

"So use a non-lethal spell."

"Even non-lethal spells might cause harm to the child she's carrying," I said. "I don't even want to knock her down with a gust of wind."

Selene sighed. "What about sneezing? Is that an acceptable risk to the child?"

"What?"

Selene leaped up onto the railing of the porch. "As usual, I have to do everything around here myself."

"Selene, don't! It's too dangerous."

The cat stretched out to her full length as she poured on the speed, becoming a gray blur across the porch. Melissa turned her gout of fire toward the speeding cat. Selene leaped into the air over the flame thrower's path and flew past Melissa's face.

As the cat sailed by, she released her secret special attack, Fur Bomb. Suddenly the air around Melissa's face swirled with little bitty, fine cat hairs that created an instant reaction in Melissa.

Melissa was overcome by a sneezing fit as she scratched at her face.

Clint saw his opening and seized her, pinning her arms to her sides before driving her carefully to the ground, ensuring she landed on her rear end, not her stomach.

"Let me go, you jerk," she snarled. Melissa kicked and squirmed furiously in his grip. She managed to get her teeth onto one of his fingers. Clint howled and released her.

I threw up all of my magic at her, creating a tornado so powerful she couldn't lift her arms to cast another blast of fire magic. The only problem was the spell wouldn't hold for long. I didn't have the magical endurance. Sweat beaded on my brow as I struggled to keep her at bay.

"Take her out already," Selene said.

"I can't!" My voice came out from behind gritted teeth. "I don't want to hurt her."

Clint was shouting something, but I couldn't hear him over the raging wind and crackling flames. He cupped his hands over his mouth and shouted until his throat went raw.

"The belly!" He shouted. I had made him out at last. "The belly!"

Yeah, of course, the belly. I knew that. That's why I was trying not to hurt Melissa ...

Then I saw it. The wind was sending Melissa's hair and clothing every which way, and when her shift lifted, I saw the "belly" was not in fact made of skin, but some kind of white foam, with a Velcro strap flapping in the wind.

"That's a horse of a different color," Selene said.

My eyes narrowed. I screamed as I poured on the power, giving it everything that I had. Melissa tried to conjure a flame, but the wind only blew it back at her, and she let out her own panicked scream before snuffing the attempted flame.

My magic was quickly draining away. I looked away only long enough to catch Clint's eye. He nodded. He was ready.

I stopped the wind and almost collapsed. Clint raced in, no longer afraid to handle Melissa roughly. He flipped her onto her fake baby bump and pinned her arms behind her back. Melissa struggled at first, but she must have been near spent, too, because the fight drained out of her quickly and her face went resolute.

Panting, I staggered over to sag against the stone sculpture before sliding down to the stamped cement driveway. "She's not really pregnant," I said, still stunned by the revelation.

"Was my brother in on this, too?" Clint asked, jabbing a finger at the fake baby bump as he kept her wrists grasped in his other hand. "Was this part of the scam? To try and get even more money somehow?"

Melissa twisted to shoot a glare over her shoulder. "It was his idea. He knew how much your mother wanted grandchildren. He thought it would help sway her to give us the money. For the baby."

Clint swore bitterly and hauled her to her feet. "Stop talking before I do something I regret."

"Of course, here we go," Selene said with a feline

sneer. "There's never a cop around when you need one, but you'd better not roll through a stop sign at four in the morning."

"What would you know about that?" I asked through shallow breaths. "You don't even drive."

"It's the principle of the thing," she insisted.

In fact, the police were on their way, thanks to Ms. Cleaver. Within a few minutes, a squad car pulled into the drive and two deputies exited the vehicle. "What's going on?" The older of the two asked, his eyes on the boneless Melissa.

"That's going to take a while to explain," I said. "But that woman murdered Seth Bridges, and tried to kill all three of us."

"Three?"

"Four of us if you count the smart-mouthed cat."

"That's better," Selene said cheerfully. Then her ears went back. "Hey!"

19

The police were most intrigued by our eyewitness accounts. Despite three witnesses fingering Melissa as the culprit, they spent the next several hours painstakingly going over the flame-damaged scene of our fight with Melissa. I gave my statement at least three times, and while I understood and respected the process, it was late, and as soon as my adrenaline crashed, my body and mind were exhausted.

Eventually they were satisfied with our accounting of the events and left us to our own devices, taking Melissa into custody.

Of course, she would still have to stand trial unless she pled out. In either case, it was going to be a hard task for a lawyer to keep her out of prison for a long, long time.

In the aftermath, Clint and I were pulled apart. The investigator wanted to speak with us one-on-one, and when they were done with him, he left the scene to go and be with his mother. She had been taken to the hospital, mostly for shock, but the paramedics who'd arrived on scene also wanted to make sure her lungs were okay. I'd seen her get carried away, on a hovering stretcher, and she'd looked gaunt and gray.

Water witches had arrived not too long after the police, and while they were able to extinguish the flames quickly, there was still extensive damage done to Clint's mother's home. I imagined she would feel another swell of panic upon returning from the hospital to the blackened ruins of her living room.

Selene and I drove home in silence, both exhausted and magically spent. For her part, Selene knew a lot of spells, but using her own limited range of powers was taxing.

When we finally settled down in my bed, I turned my head to the feline lounging on the pillow beside mine. "Perhaps the most shocking confession of all was yours," I teased. "Since when have you ever wanted to sit on my lap?"

The cat didn't bother lifting her head. "You know, I think your candle may have been malfunctioning."

"Really? That is most peculiar, considering how well it worked on Melissa."

"Maybe it works differently for cats. Like, instead of making us blurt out our heart's desire, we blurt out the exact opposite. Did you ever think of that?"

"I guess I should refine my mix a little bit."

"Yeah, you probably should."

That was the last word on it, but I still felt better thinking that Selene maybe did not despise me as much as she indicated. Somehow, over the past few weeks, I'd kind of got used to her being around. Without a snarky cat, I think my house might start to feel pretty empty, indeed.

When sleep came for me, it dragged me down deep, and I slept better than I had in a long time. I awoke the next morning with more energy than I'd expected to have, though I could feel my magical reserves were still weakened. That wasn't an overnight fix.

Selene was still snoozing when I rolled out of bed. I went to the kitchen to start my coffee, and while I waited, I washed and dried Selene's bowl. Afterward, I checked on the status of her Cyber-

Litter 5000, and found it was scheduled to be delivered later that day.

When Selene padded out to join me, she went to her bowl and sniffed at the serving of soft food. "Hey, did you wash my bowl?"

"Yes, I did. No need to thank me."

"Thank you? You did a crummy job."

Frowning, I paused mid–pancake flip. "Selene, that bowl was spotless when I finished with it. You know it, and I know it."

"Is it clean? Yes, I cannot dispute that. However, you don't seem to realize how sensitive my nose truly is. All I can smell is the stench of the dish liquid you used to clean it. Either switch to unscented, or next time, just use hot water and a little elbow grease. Capisce?"

"I'll keep that in mind for next time," I said, rolling my eyes as I turned back to fixing my own breakfast.

Selene looked up at me. "Are you sick or something?"

"No, I'm fine. Why?"

"You're just being very … agreeable," she replied, her whiskers twitching suspiciously.

I smiled at her, and it blew her little kitty mind.

After breakfast, I dressed and headed to Wicked

Wicks. Considering the events of the night before, no one would have blamed me if I'd decided to take the day off, but I didn't want to disappoint my regulars. On top of that, I needed the routine of it all. Otherwise, I would sit at home all day replaying the confrontation with Melissa over and over again.

My morning rush made the early hours fly past. By the time it was slow enough I could eat my lunch, I'd already jotted down half a dozen candles that would need to be restocked when I got a chance.

Naturally, I'd been checking my phone all day in between customers, hoping to hear from Clint. As the day wore on, my concern grew. I started to wonder if there had been some kind of complication with his mother at the hospital, especially in light of what she'd told him about her diagnosis.

I was about to break down and call him when he suddenly appeared, walking by the display window of my shop. I almost hadn't recognized him, seeing as he was dressed down for once, in a pair of jeans and a t-shirt. A thin layer of stubble also coated his jawline. If anything, he only looked more handsome this way. I'd never been a huge suit-and-tie girl, anyway. Jeans, bedhead, and a soft cotton tee was just fine with me.

Clint opened the door and stepped into my shop,

bearing two paper bags, both handles in one hand, while his other was busy carrying a cardboard drink carrier with two cups of coffee.

Selene perked up right away. "What did you bring, Clinton my boy?"

He arched a brow at her use of his hated full name but didn't offer complaint as he set the drink carrier on the front counter. "I stopped by the coffee shop *and* the fish market."

Selene's eyes went huge. "The fish market?"

He smiled and set a bag down beside her so she could take a big sniff. "It's my way of saying thank you for helping to clear my name," he said. His smile faded, and his eyes grew somber. "I wouldn't have gotten very far without you, Cora."

"What am I, chopped liver?"

"Of course not," Clint said, giving her a little scritch behind the ears.

"Hey, you can't—" Her protests died as he moved his fingers to get the sweet spot under her chin.

I laughed and peeked into the other bag. Inside were two fully loaded bagels. Not quite as good as a dragon's hoard cookie, but I'd take it. "You really didn't have to do this," I said.

"No, I did," Clint replied, ceasing his petting of

Selene—who actually seemed a bit grumpy as his hand drifted away from her.

"How is your mother?" I asked.

He exhaled. "Shaken, of course, but I think she'll be all right. She's booked in a suite at the Winterspell Chalet until the fire damage is cleaned up and repaired."

"I'm glad she's all right," I said.

Clint bobbed his head.

"So, what are your plans now? You're a free man, and can leave Winterspell whenever you want, right?"

"Actually, I think I'm going to stick around for a while," he said.

"Oh yeah?" I tried to keep my voice sounding casual, but a little bit of optimism crept in. "Why is that?"

"Well, I really don't want to leave my mother alone right now." His eyes grew somber. "She's … she's been through a lot. First, she loses her son, and then she finds her daughter-in-law is a liar, and worse a killer, and the grandson she'd been waiting for turned out to be as fake as the marriage."

I cocked an eyebrow. "I wonder what Melissa thought was going to happen when it was time for her to deliver that grandchild."

Clint's jaw worked silently for a long moment. "I think … I think, given Mom's declining health, she thought there was a good possibility … that is, that my mother wouldn't be around for the delivery anyway."

I felt a stab of sympathy. "Oh, Seth and Melissa knew about the diagnosis?"

"They've known for a few months," Clint said with a slight nod. "We had a long talk this morning, about everything. There's still a long way to go toward repairing our relationship, but if there is a chance I can make things better before she—well, you understand."

"Of course I do." My heart welled with empathy for both him and his mother. I didn't know the full history and considering my own family could not be more different than his, I wasn't sure I could ever truly understand it, but I knew his pain was real and imagined his mother's was as well.

"I'm so sorry, Clint. After all that's happened—" I broke off and shook my head slowly.

"She has me to help take care of her now." Clint's smile returned. "Besides, nothing's set in stone, right?"

"Right."

"I guess losing my brother has shown me that

family is important. Far more important than the way I've treated it these past years." He heaved a long sigh. "I sometimes wonder if part of what happened to Seth isn't my fault."

"Why on Earth would it be your fault?"

"Because I drifted away from my family. If I'd been keeping in contact, doing what brothers are supposed to do … maybe I could have talked him out of the fake marriage scheme. Maybe we could have come to some compromise. I could have shown him that I wasn't a threat to the inheritance money."

"You can't blame yourself, Clint."

He offered a grateful smile, but I could tell it wasn't the last of the battle with his own conscience. For better or worse, he'd have to work that part out for himself.

"So, what about your business?" I asked, trying to avoid an awkward silence.

"I can work remotely," he said with a shrug. "It's the internet age. Thanks to Wi-Fi, my office is wherever I want it to be."

"Yeah, and if something happens to your laptop, you can always steal Cora's again," Selene offered.

"Selene …" I sighed.

Clint chuckled softly. "No, she's right." He shook

his head, still smiling. "I can't believe you put up with me all this time."

"I'm happy I was able to help," I said, and meant it.

"There is one thing that's still bothering me," he said.

"What's that?"

"Do you remember the first day we met?"

"It would be a little hard to forget," I answered with a laugh. "You asked me to dinner, and then my ex-husband showed up."

"Well, we never did get to have that dinner." Clint straightened. "So, what do you say? Can we try this again?"

My heart skipped a beat. "Yes, I'd be delighted."

"Great." He glanced at his phone when it dinged. "That's Mother's lawyer. I should take this."

"I understand. Take care of her."

He took one of the coffee cups from the holder, and as he turned to leave, he hoisted it up and smiled. "I'll be back at closing time though. If that works for you?"

I laughed. "I'll be here."

"I'm really looking forward to it, Cora." He paused at the door to look back at me for a long moment. Something passed between us, and I felt the stirrings of that initial rush of excitement I'd had upon our first meeting.

I returned to my workday, distracted by a fresh run of customers coming through the door. Still, Clint remained at the forefront of my mind.

"Solve a murder, get a boyfriend," Selene said later that day. "Not bad for a week's work."

"He's not my boyfriend," I said quickly, cheeks flushing hot. "We're just going to dinner."

"Uh huh. Well, then you shouldn't have a problem telling Roger about it."

"Ugh," I sighed. "Did you have to bring up my ex-husband? I was trying to enjoy the moment."

"Well, I thought I should, since he just pulled up outside."

"He did?" On some kind of autopilot, I found myself brushing fingers through my hair and tidying up my apron a bit as I watched Roger cross the street and head for my front door.

The bell rang, and he smiled as he walked inside. "Hello, Cora."

"Hello, Roger," I said with a note of resignation as the now-familiar swirl of turmoil kicked up in my gut. "What brings you in today?"

"I wanted to see how you were doing." He walked up to the counter and stopped. "I was at Sugar Shack this morning, picking up a few things, and I heard a couple of witches talking about you. They were saying you got into a fight with a fire witch, and the police were called. What happened?"

"It's a long story, but it's true. I'm okay, though."

"Thank goodness," he exclaimed, though I caught him scanning my bare arms for any sign of harm anyway. "Wow. I bet you could use a little TLC, after all that. What do you think about me cooking you dinner tonight? We could watch a movie—your choice, and—"

"Um, listen, Roger." I sighed. "I don't know what more I can really say, but I'm not comfortable with the idea of having dinner with you. Even as friends. It just seems … loaded."

"There's no chance you'll change your mind?"

"I don't think so." I paused and looked down at the coffee cup in front of me. Clint's name was written on the side in permanent ink.

Roger noticed and let out a sigh. "Ah. I see." He swallowed hard, but then nodded. "I hope he makes you happy, Cora. I truly do. You deserve the very best."

"Thank you, Roger. That means a lot to me."

I came out from behind the counter and offered him an embrace. He held me tight, and for a moment, I was transported back to another time and place. When I stepped out of his arms, a ball of emotion had crawled into my throat. "Maybe we could have coffee sometime," I acquiesced. "As friends."

Roger smiled. "I'd really like that."

"Okay."

He headed back to the door and I waved. "See you around, Roger."

"See you, Cora."

20

I spent the rest of the day in a tug-of-war with my emotions: burgeoning hope over the new possibilities with Clint, and melancholy reminiscing over memories made with Roger. Selene had managed to eat her entire thank-you gift from Clint and was sleeping it off in the back room of the shop, leaving me to my own wandering thoughts. Business trickled off as the afternoon turned to evening, and I was able to distract myself somewhat by whipping up a few custom orders.

There were thirty minutes to closing left when I decided I had time to do one more. It was a Treasured Memories candle, meant to conjure happy nostalgia for the user. Another version of the same base candle, meant to invoke painful memories of the past, was typically only used under the guidance of a mental health professional, sort of like a version of hypnosis meant to aid in trauma recovery. Luckily, it didn't seem there was a huge demand for that version of the candle in Winterspell. Still, I had to be careful in the crafting of the candle itself, because a mistake could lead to the opposite intended effect taking place upon burning the wick.

I poured light green melted wax into the long, tapered mold and left it to cool while I gathered the components for the happy memories spell. It was critical that I cast the spell into the wax just as it hardened fully.

The material components for the spell are, like most other spell components, decidedly symbolic. Were I a scientist, I would use a bit of brain or something, but I'm not a scientist. I'm a witch.

So, when I say that the chief component for the spell was a stopwatch that had stopped running on its own volition, you will pardon the confusion. I examined the watch in the palm of my hand. It felt heavy, almost ponderous. The glass face plate featured a noticeable crack running down the middle.

I could go into a long diatribe on why it has to be a watch that has stopped of its own volition. If I were to take a watch and physically damage it so it would not function, then that would spoil the spell. This is because memories have to flow naturally and don't do well when you try to force them.

The next component of the spell was a hawk feather. This had nothing to do with memories, but rather was a token of my being a wind witch. The feather represented the element of air.

Finally, I needed a bit of pixie dust. The pixies in Winterspell exuded it naturally, and the enterprising ones swept up their homes and businesses and compiled the dust for merchandising purposes.

Why pixie dust? Pixies never forget. Non-magics say it's elephants with ironclad memories, but that's only because non-magics have never met a pixie before.

Once I'd gathered all the components for my spell, I focused on the casting. I used a bit of wind to carry the watch, dust, and feather aloft into a swirling cyclone.

I chanted the words to the spell as the lights flickered overhead. The eldritch fabric of the universe bent to my whims as I shaped the very essence of reality—

Until I inhaled deeply and sucked a bit of gray cat fluff up my nose.

I sneezed twice as I swiped at my face, trying to rid it of any further stray hairs. "That darn cat," I gasped as I reached for a tissue. I wiped my watery eyes, then opened them to resume the spell—

Only to find it had already finished. I cursed myself silently as the material components—joined by a bit of cat fluff—swirled in a cyclone over the nearly hardened candle.

"Oh no," I muttered as clock, pixie dust, feather, and cat dander all congealed into the wax.

The candle's gorgeous light green color darkened into something black as midnight, black as pitch, blacker than the foulest witch …

Well, it wasn't completely black. There were these little gold flecks in it that caught the light in a pleasing way. Then I realized that the gold flecks weren't just reflecting light but producing it.

They say many great discoveries were by accident. I feared the worst from what my carelessness had wrought.

I sighed and rubbed the bridge of my nose. I would have to start all over from scratch. I set the black and gold candle aside and drew out my gear for the next casting. I was lucky I'd acquired a whole box of broken watches from a yard sale a few years back.

As I set about creating the new candle, Selene came into the front of the shop, pausing for a long stretch in the arched doorway. "What time is it?"

I gave her a bemused smile. "Morning, Sleeping Beauty."

"Morning?" the cat repeated with a panicked look.

"No, it's not—I was just—oh, never mind." I sighed and glanced at the clock. "It's fifteen minutes to closing time."

"What in the heck is that?" Selene leaped onto the counter and sniffed the black candle I had accidentally created. "This isn't one of your usual models, is it?"

"No, it definitely isn't one of my usual models."

"For some reason, I truly believe this is the most fantastic, wonderful thing you've ever created." Her nose wriggled as she sniffed the candle. "Hey, it smells like me!"

I explained the mishap to Selene. Not only did she find it quite amusing, she seemed to think it was destiny.

"Ah, the fickle finger of fate has intervened, and helped you to create something truly wondrous. Light it for me. Put those opposable thumbs to good use."

"You want me to light it?" I frowned at the candle. "I don't know if that's such a good idea. I have no idea what kind of effect it will have."

"Who knows? You trapped some of my essence in the spell. It could wind up cloning me. Wouldn't that be great? Two Selenes."

I shuddered to think.

"Wouldn't that make you less unique?" I asked, peering at her from over the candle's wick.

"I've often thought the world would be a better, saner place if *all* witches were replaced with versions of me."

"You would," I muttered. "Fine, I'll light it, but it's only a memory candle. It's not likely to clone you or give you superpowers."

"We don't know that for sure."

I sighed and lit the candle. At first, nothing happened other than a brief curling tendril of black smoke and the smell of burned cat hair. Then, Selene's eyes went wide.

"What's wrong?"

"I'm having a memory," Selene gasped. "A lost memory. It's of Lavender!"

"Lavender?" I cocked an eyebrow. "What kind of memory?"

"Nothing much. It looks pretty boring. She's just

puttering around in her house looking at—oh no. Lavender, look out!"

"What's going on?" My fear spiked at the urgency in Selene's tone.

"There's a masked man—I mean, I think it's a man, it could be a woman—sneaking up behind her. Turn around! Fry that fool with lightning!"

Selene winced.

"What happened?" I demanded, wishing I could see the memory as well.

"The assailant just hit her with a spell. The magic was blue. *Silvery* blue."

"What kind of spell?"

"I—I don't know." Selene's eyes widened once more.

"What's happening now?"

"Lavender is limp as a rag doll, and the one in black is carrying her out of the house, through the kitchen door—" She paused, her eyes falling closed. She gave a shake of her head, then looked up at me, her gaze haunted. "That's all I could see. The memory is gone."

The candle went out, and I felt a chill run down my spine. I grabbed my phone. I had to call my mother, right that second. Aunt Lavender wasn't on an adventure. She'd been kidnapped.

WHAT HAS HAPPENED to Aunt Lavender? The adventure continues in Hexed Hiss-tory, book two in the Nine Lives Magic series.

Get back to Winterspell today!

If you'd like to know what it was like when Selene first came to live with Cora, you can join my newsletter and receive a free copy of the short story, A Tail of Nine Lives Magic.

www.DanielleGarrettBooks.com/newsletter

If you'd like to chat with me on come join the Bat Wings Book Club on Facebook. It's my happy little corner of the internet and I love chatting with readers and sharing behind the scenes fun.

IF YOU'D LIKE to spend more time in Winterspell, check out the original series set in this magical town. Sprinkles and Sea Serpents is full of sweet treats, sassy cats, and a talking sea monster! *Find the Sugar Shack Witch Mysteries on Amazon.*

UNTIL NEXT TIME, **happy reading!**
   Danielle Garrett
   www.DanielleGarrettBooks.com

ALSO BY DANIELLE GARRETT

One town. Two spunky leading ladies.
More magic than you can shake a wand at.
Welcome to Beechwood Harbor.

Come join the fun in Beechwood Harbor, the little town where witches, shifters, ghosts, and vamps all live, work, play, and—mostly—get along!

The two main series set in this world are the Beechwood Harbor Magic Mysteries and the Beechwood Harbor Ghost Mysteries.

In the following pages you will find more information about those books, as well as my other works available.

Alternatively, you can find a complete reading list on my website:

www.DanielleGarrettBooks.com

SUGAR SHACK WITCH MYSTERIES

In Winterspell Lake there are things darker than midnight...

Sprinkles and Sea Serpents is the first book in a brand new paranormal cozy mystery series by Danielle Garrett. This series features magic, mystery, family squabbles, sassy heroines, and a mysterious monster hunter—all with a little sugar sprinkled on top.

Find the Sugar Shack Witch Mysteries on Amazon.

ABOUT THE AUTHOR

Danielle Garrett has been an avid bookworm for as long as she can remember, immersing herself in the magic of far-off places and the rich lives of witches, wizards, princesses, elves, and some wonderful everyday heroes as well. Her love of reading naturally blossomed into a passion for storytelling, and today, she's living the dream she's nurtured since the second grade—crafting her own worlds and characters as an author.

A proud Oregonian, Danielle loves to travel but always finds her way back to the Pacific Northwest, where she shares her life with her husband and their beloved menagerie of animal companions.

Visit Danielle today at her website or say "hello" on Facebook.

www.DanielleGarrettBooks.com

Made in United States
Cleveland, OH
03 December 2024